The Rip Van Winkle Caper

"All right. Check your airlocks first, gentlemen."

The other three men followed his directions, and then three sets of eyes turned in their confinement to look across the cave toward the first coffin.

"Now begin to count," Farwell's voice said, "and on ten, release the gas." The lips of the four men moved as the quiet countdown took place—then, very slowly into each glass enclosure came a white stream of milky gas until the bodies inside were no longer visible.

"Good night, gentlemen." Farwell's voice was heavy and indistinct.

"Pleasant dreams and a good sleep. I'll see you . . . in the next century." His voice became weaker. "In the next century, gentlemen."

WHAT DID THEY DISCOVER WHEN THEY AWOKE? WHAT YOU ALWAYS FIND IN THE TWILIGHT ZONE—A STRANGE, IMPROBABLE WORLD FRAUGHT WITH DANGER AND SUSPENSE.

ROD SERLING, best known for his classic series "The Twilight Zone" and "Night Gallery," was one of the most highly respected writers of eerie fantasy. A six-time Emmy-winner for such teleplays as "Requiem for a Heavyweight" and "The Comedians," his stories touch a chord deep in the heart of our darkest fears.

NEW STORIES FROM THE TWILIGHT ZONE

Rod Serling

BANTAM BOOKS
Toronto • New York • London • Sydney

RL 5, IL age 13 and up

NEW STORIES FROM THE TWILIGHT ZONE
A Bantam Book / May 1962

2nd printing ..... *May 1962*	*4th printing* .. *November 1962*
3rd printing .... *August 1962*	*5th printing* ...... *July 1964*
6th printing ... *September 1964*	

Bantam Pathfinder edition / July 1965

8th printing .. *October 1965*	*13th printing* .. *January 1970*
9th printing ... *August 1966*	*14th printing* ..... *May 1971*
10th printing ..... *June 1967*	*15th printing* . *December 1971*
11th printing . *November 1967*	*16th printing* . *November 1972*
12th printing ..... *July 1969*	*17th printing* . *September 1973*
18th printing ... *October 1974*	

Bantam edition / December 1975

20th printing ..... *July 1976*	*22nd printing* ..... *May 1982*
21st printing . *December 1978*	*23rd printing* ..... *July 1983*

ISBN 0-553-22782-3

Published simultaneously in the United States and Canada

PRINTED IN THE UNITED STATES OF AMERICA

H   32 31 30 29 28 27 26 25 24 23

CONTENTS

THE
WHOLE
TRUTH

YOU could say this of Harvey Henni-
cutt—he was an exceptional liar. When Harvey peddled one
of his used cars, his lying was colorful, imaginative, and had a
charm all of its own.

Along automobile row it was said of him that he could
sell anything that had at least two wheels, one headlight, one
unbroken glass, and a semblance of an engine—given ten
minutes to make the pitch. Many of his most famous trans-
actions are doubtless apocryphal, but some of them are
quite authentic, because I remember them myself.

There was the time he latched on to the old General
Sherman tank. Bought it off a junk dealer for twenty-five
dollars. Harvey put it on a big wooden platform in front of
his lot and offered it as the "Week's Special." Now, you may
well ask who in their right mind would buy a fifty-three-ton
General Sherman tank, complete with cannon. Most of the
scoffers along the row posed the same question. But Harvey
had picked up the vehicle on Thursday, and by Friday
morning, at 9:12, he had sold it for three hundred and
eighty-six dollars!

I happened to be in the neighborhood that morning and I
heard part of his pitch: "Ever see a buggy like this? Take this
little baby out on the highway and see what kinda courtesy you
get! No teenager's gonna try to fender-bender ya with this
one! Depreciation? Why, hell! I know four members of the
Joint Chiefs of Staff and a C.I.A. guy who drives these
things regularly back and forth to the Pentagon. The styles
don't change, so it ain't never obsolete—and you know how
efficient a diesel engine is. The cannon? It's the most effective
turn signal you could ever use. The guy behind you has
gotta be blind or three days dead not to notice it! Snow, ice,
rain, muck, sleet, hail—why, hell, man!—this thing'll go in
any weather. Look at the way it's built. What other car on the

1

road has six and a half inches of bullet-proof armor? Visibility? You mean the slit there—in front of where the driver sits? Why, that makes you keep your eye on the road. Nothin' to detract you—no road signs, scenery, good-lookin' broads in sports cars, or anything else. 'Cause all you see is the road right smack dab in front of ya. Why, hell! If I could've latched onto ten of these during prohibition, I could've retired long ago!"

The buyer was a mild little mailman who had simply dropped by the lot to deliver two circulars and a letter from Harvey's aunt. He drove off in the General Sherman tank, looking a little benumbed by the whole thing—and Harvey Hennicutt watched him pull out and stood at rigid attention, saluting, as the thing rumbled by.

Harvey wasn't an innately dishonest man. He didn't lie because he was some kind of devious bastard. It was just that his entire frame of reference was "the deal." He had to buy, sell, and trade the way most people find it necessary to breathe. It was not the extra sixty-five bucks he ootzed out of a hapless customer, but simply the principle of backing someone up against a wall and then slowly bending his opponent's will until it dissolved. In the twenty-odd years I knew Harvey, I never heard him tell a stupid lie. They were all of them bright, well conceived, and rather pure, as lies go. All of which leads to the story that he told me when last I saw him.

Now, normally most of Harvey's stories can be overlooked —but not this one. The Harvey Hennicutt who buttonholed me out in front of his lot on that grey, sullen November day was a different man, and a different storyteller. Even the loud, garish sport coat that was his uniform and that screeched at you with its off-violet checks, the flamboyant hand-painted tie, the Stetson sitting on the back of his head could not disguise the grim, set, almost frightened look on Harvey's face. And this was his story:

It was in September—a beautiful Indian summer late afternoon. A golden sun sparkled through the somewhat faded bunting that surrounded Harvey's used-car emporium. It highlighted one particular banner that read: "Harvey Hennicutt's Used Motors—Not a Dud in the Lot." And there stood the cars—or rather, "lay" the cars. Because Harvey's stock in trade was, and always had been, the antique lemon barely able to wheeze on and off his lot. Harvey was leaning against a car, cleaning his nails and watching a young couple examining a 1928 Buick at the far end of the lot.

You had to see Harvey's face to believe it on an occasion like this. He was a General of the Armies deciding the strategy of the attack. He was the psychiatrist analyzing the patient. Now he put on his most infectious smile—the one he saved up for the initial assault, and he carried it with him over to the antique Buick.

The young man looked up somewhat diffidently and nervously.

"We were just looking—"

"We want you to!" Harvey exclaimed. "We certainly want you to. Nobody rushes you around here. Nossir, young man, around here you can exhale, pause, check and re-check, think, peruse, contemplate, thumb over, wade through, and dip into." He made an expansive gesture at the line of cars. "Be my guest, folks."

The young man and woman blinked as the verbal wave hit them and bowled them over.

"We were . . ." the young man began hesitantly. "We were thinking of . . . you know . . . a nice four-door. Something under five hundred dollars and as late a model as we could go."

Harvey closed his eyes, shook his head with a pained, desperate expression on his face. "You shock me, do you know that?" He then looked toward the girl. "Did you know that your husband shocked me just then?"

The girl's mouth formed an O, and then plopped closed. Harvey tapped the fender of the old car.

"Do you know why you shocked me?" he asked. "Do you? I'll tell you why you shocked me. Because you have succumbed to the propaganda of every cement-headed clod up and down this street. I said *propaganda*!" He pounded on the car and left a dent which he hurriedly covered up with his elbow. "They tell ya to go with the late models. Don't they? They do, don't they?"

Captivated, the young man and woman nodded in unison.

"You know *why* they tell ya to go with the late models?" Harvey continued. "Do you think they do that because they're honest, law-abiding, rigidly moral church-goers?" He shook his head and made a face like a minister suddenly observing a crap game in one of the pews. "Let me tell ya something, young man." He waggled a finger in the young man's face. "They push late models because that's where the profit margin is! They'll try to cram the post-fifty-fours down your gullet because they'd rather make a buck than a friend! They'd rather make a profit than a relationship!"

Again he pounded on the fender, forgetting himself—and this time there was the screech of metal as the fender separated from the body of the car. Harvey hid this disaster by deliberately standing in front of it.

"They would rather fill their wallets with cash, than their hearts with the fellowship of men to men," Harvey continued.

The young man gulped and swallowed. "Well, all we're looking for is good transportation, and we figured that the newer the car—"

Harvey threw up his hands, interrupting him. "Now, that's where you're wrong! That is precisely where you have gone amiss. That is the juncture where you have headed off into a blind alley. You don't want a new car. You don't want one of these rinky-dinks slapped together on an assembly line, covered with chintzy chrome, fin tails, idiotic names, and no more workmanship than you can stick into a thimble! I'll tell ya what you're lookin' for." Again he pointed a waggling finger into the young man's face. "What you're lookin' for is the craftsmanship that comes with age! The dependability that comes with a proven performance! The dignity of traditional transportation."

He drew back as if unveiling the Hope diamond, and pointed to the car behind him. "This is what you're lookin' for. This is a 1938 four-door Chevy—and this will get ya where ya want to go and get ya back."

Harvey's voice went on and on. The pitch took another four or five minutes. And while the whole thing sounded spontaneous it was all a practiced routine. He broke down his assault into three phases. First was the slam bang, "back-'em-up-against-a-wall" for the initial contact. The second phase was the one he entered into now—the quiet, rather beneficent, patient phase. Later came part three, the wrap-up. Right now, he smiled beatifically at the two young people, winked at the girl as if to say, "I've got a few little ones like you at home myself"—and then, in a voice much gentler, pointed to the Chevy.

"Look. I don't want to rush you kids. Rushing isn't my business. Satisfaction happens to be my business. And I tell ya what ya do. Spend some time with that automobile. Look it over. Sit in it. Get the feel of it. Relish the luxury of it. Check and see how they built cars when cars were really built. Go ahead, my friend," he continued, leading the young man over to the front door—and then hurriedly reaching out to grab the wife. "Sit in it. Climb right in there and sit to your heart's content. What you really need is some candle-light and a good bottle of wine. Because this baby right here has dignity!"

Harvey heard the sound of a car pulling into the lot at the far end. He slammed the door on the young couple, rais-ing a cloud of dust and an agonized groan of protesting metal, smiled at his victims through the cloudy glass, and then hurried over to the north end of the lot where other com-merce appeared to be waiting for him.

The "commerce" in this case was a model A Ford, driven by a silvery-haired old man with a face like Santa Claus and happy, guileless eyes. Harvey had a thing about happy, guile-less eyes, because it usually meant a quick, and relatively painless, transaction. He walked up within a few feet of the model A. It chugged, whinnied, backfired twice, and finally came to an uneasy stop. The old man got out and smiled at Harvey.

"How do you do?"

Harvey ran a tongue around the inside of his mouth. "That depends, grandpa. If you're here to park it—I'll charge you nominal rates. If you're here to sell it—you've gotta give me three and a half minutes to have my little laugh." With this, he stepped back and surveyed the car, tilting his head in several different directions, walking around several times with an occasional look at the old man. Finally he stopped, heaved a deep sigh, put his hands behind his back, and closed his eyes for a moment.

"Well?" the old man asked quietly.

"I might give ya fifteen bucks. A junk yard'll give ya twelve, and the Smithsonian might beat us both by a buck or two."

The old man merely smiled a gentle smile. "It's a wonder-ful old car and they made them better in the old days, I think . . ."

Harvey's eyes rolled wildly, and he shook his head as if struggling for an almost superhuman patience. "Grandfather dear," he said, holding out his hands in a gesture of resigna-tion, "that is the old rhubarb. The saw. The turkey that everybody and his brother tries to peddle on the open market." Then, mimicking fiercely: " 'Cars were built better in the old days.' That, sir, is a fabrication beyond belief! Why, ten years ago they didn't know how to build cars. It's the new stuff that sells. It's the new stuff that runs. It's the new stuff that shows the genius of mind, muscle, and the assembly line!"

He very condescendingly, and with a kind of super-secretive air, leaned toward the old man. "I'll tell ya what I'll do—because I love your face." He made a motion encompassing the man's whole figure. "Because you remind me of my own grandfather, rest his soul. A man of dignity right down through his twilight years till the day he died saving a boatload of capsized people on the East River!" His eyes went down reverently for a moment, and then up again very quickly. "I'll give ya twenty-five for it. I'll probably have to dismantle it and sell it wheel by wheel, bolt by bolt, to whatever itinerant junk man comes around. But twenty-five I'll give ya!"

"Twenty-five dollars?" The old man looked at the car with nostalgia. "I . . . I kind of need the money." He turned to Harvey. "You couldn't make it thirty?"

Harvey stuck a cold cigar between his teeth and looked away. "You try me, old friend," he said in a grim voice. "You try me right down to the bare nerve of my most inveterate patience!"

The old man kept looking at Harvey. "Does that mean—" he tried to interject.

Harvey smiled down at him with the same assaulted patience. "That means that twenty-five is going, going, going . . . twenty-five is gone!" With a single motion, his wallet was out of his hip pocket, and from a cash-packed interior, he removed three bills and handed them to the old man. He turned him around and pointed toward the shack in the center of the lot.

"You walk into that little office there," he ordered, "and bring your car registration papers with you." He looked toward the model A. "Did I say 'car'? I meant . . ." He wiggled his fingers as though searching for a word. "That vehicle! I'll stretch a point as far as the next man! But there are limits, my charming old friend, there are definitely limits." With this, he turned abruptly and walked away, back to the young couple still seated in the 1938 Chevy.

He peered at them through the window, wiggled his fingers, smiled, winked, ran a tongue over his teeth, and then looked skyward with suppressed impatience. In the process, he propped a foot on the rear bumper of the car and it immediately clattered to the ground. Harvey lifted it back into place, secured it with a kick, and then turned to walk over to the shack.

When he went inside, the old man had just finished with the registration papers. He smiled at Harvey. "Signed, sealed, and delivered, Mr. . . ." He looked out of the window toward the giant banner. "Mr. Hennicutt. Here are the keys." He placed a set of ignition keys on the desk, and stared at them for a reflective moment. Then he looked at Harvey with a small, apologetic smile. "There is one other item that I ought to mention to you about the car."

Harvey was examining the registration papers and barely looked up. "Oh—do, do," he said.

"It's haunted."

Harvey looked up at him briefly and gave a kind of "see-what-I-have-to-go-through" smile. "Is that a fact?"

"Oh, yes," the old man said. "Indubitably. The car is haunted. It's been haunted since the day it came off the assembly line, and every single one of its owners can attest to this fact."

Harvey continued to smile as he walked around the desk and sat down in his chair. He winked, puckered up his mouth, ran his tongue around inside his cheeks. His voice was quite gentle. "I don't suppose you'd like to tell me," he asked, "*how* the car is haunted . . . or how I can get it unhaunted?"

"Oh, you'll find out soon enough," the old man said. He rose and started for the door. "And as for unhaunting it— you'll have to sell the car. Good day to you, Mr. Hennicutt. It's been a pleasure doing business with you."

Harvey remained seated in his chair. "Oh, likewise . . . likewise," he said.

The old man paused at the door and turned to him. "I think you'll find that you may have actually gotten the best of the bargain at that."

Harvey laced his fingers together behind his head. "My aged friend," he announced in a hurt tone, "you do me the ultimate injustice. This little transaction, haunted or otherwise, is my charity case of the day. You dwell on that, will you? Just go ahead and dwell on it."

The old man pursed his lips. "No, no, no, Mr. Hennicutt. *You* dwell on it— And I rather think you will." Then he laughed, and walked out of the office.

Harvey looked down at the registration papers, then shoved them untidily into a basket on his desk, already running over in his mind how he could advertise the model A as one of the cars used on the "Untouchables"—or even, perhaps, plugging it as the actual car used by Eliot Ness in his capture of Baby Face Floyd. He'd shoot a couple of .22 holes in the rear fender and point these out as having taken place during the monumental chase. Three hundred bucks easy for a car with this history and tradition of law and order. His daydreaming was stopped by the sound of the young couple's voices approaching from outside. He looked out the window to see them walking toward the shack. He immediately replaced his normal expression of avarice by his "third-phase, wrap-'em-up" look—a mixture of parental affection and rock-ribbed, almost painful, honesty. It was this look he took outside with him.

The young man pointed to a 1934 Auburn. "How much is that one over there?" he inquired.

A pigeon, Harvey thought. An absolute, unadulterated, bonafide, A-number-one honest-to-God pigeon. That Auburn had been with Harvey for twelve years. It was the first automobile and the last one he'd ever lost money on. He cleared his throat. "You mean that collectors' item? That's —that's—" Harvey's eyes bugged. For some crazy reason, nothing more came out. He formed the words—packed them up like snowballs, and tried to throw them, *but nothing came out!*

After a moment something did come out. It was Harvey's voice and they were his words, but he was not conscious of actually saying them. "It's not for sale," his voice said.

The young man exchanged a look with his wife and then pointed to a Chevy that had been sitting there. "How about the Chev?"

Again Harvey felt his mouth open—and again he heard his voice. "That one's not for sale either."

"Not for sale?" The young man looked at him strangely. "But that's the one you were pushing."

"That's the one I was pushing," Harvey's voice said—and this time he knew he was saying it—"but I'm not pushing it any more. That's a heap! A rum-dum. It hasn't got any rings. It hasn't got any plugs. It hasn't got any points. It's got a cracked block and it'll eat up gasoline like it owned every oil well in the state of Texas."

Harvey's eyes looked glazed and he made a massive effort to close his mouth, but still the words came out of it. "The rubber's gone and the chassis' bent, and if I ever referred to it as a runabout, what I meant by that was that it'll run about a mile and then stop. It'll cost you double what you paid for it the minute you try to get it repaired—and you'll be gettin' it repaired every third Thursday of the month."

The young couple stared at him incredulously and Harvey stared back. His tongue felt like a red-hot poker in his mouth. He stood there forlornly, wondering when this madness would pass from him. The young couple exchanged yet another look, and finally the young man stammered, "Well . . . well, what else have you got?"

Harvey's words came out despite anything he could do to stop them. "I haven't anything to show you that's worth your while," he announced. "Everything I've got on this lot should have been condemned years ago. I've got more lemons per square foot than the United Fruit Company. So, my advice to you kids would be to run along and head for a reputable place where you get what you pay for and be pleased with it, but don't come around here, because I'll rob you blind!"

The young man was about to retort when his wife gave him a sharp nudge with her elbow, motioned with her head, and the two of them walked away.

Harvey remained standing there, absolutely motionless. He found himself drawn to the model A that stood in plain, simple, almost exquisite, homeliness. Harvey blinked, shook himself like a big St. Bernard, and then deliberately, with conscious effort, walked back into the shack.

He sat inside for several hours, asking himself a hundred times just what the hell had happened. It was as if some demon had entered him, fastened itself to his larynx and dictated his language. It was the screwiest odd-ball feeling he'd ever felt. But several hours later the feeling had worn off. What the hell, Harvey thought to himself, what the hell! They looked like the kind of kids who'd be back in the morning, screaming for their money.

But once again, for perhaps the twentieth time, he let his eyes rest on the model A. Haunted, the old man had said. Haunted! God damn you, Harvey Hennicutt, you will persist in dealing with kooks.

A few moments later, Harvey's assistant entered the shack. This was a sallow post-teenager named Irving Proxmier. Irving was an undernourished version of his master, affecting the same sport coat, the hat tilted on the back of his head, and a hand-painted tie that showed a hula dancer under a Hawaiian setting sun. But the imitation, of course, was noticeably inferior to the original. The effort showed itself, but only the effort.

"Sorry I'm late, boss," Irving announced, putting a cigar in his teeth in exactly the same manner he'd watched Harvey do it. "I was checking the junk yard for those '34 Chevy wheel disks. I found two of them." He looked behind him through the open door. "What's the action?"

Harvey blinked. "A little quiet this afternoon." Then, shaking himself from his deep reflections, he pointed out the window. "That '35 Essex, Irv. I want you to push that one."

"Push it is right. It'll never get any place under its own power."

Harvey lit a cigar. "Knock it down to fifty-five bucks. Tell everybody it's a museum piece. The last of its kind." He rose from the chair, walked over to the open door and peered outside. He noticed then that the hood of the Essex was partially open. "Boobie," he announced grievously, "you gotta close the hood, boobie." He turned to Irving. "How many times I gotta tell ya that? When ya can't see the engine for the rust—you've gotta play a little hide-and-seek. You don't go advertisin' the fact that you're tryin' to job off a car that carried French soldiers to the first Battle of the Marne."

Harvey's face suddenly looked very white. His lower lip sagged. That strange haunted look appeared in his eyes. He whirled around and retraced his steps over to the desk. "Irv," he said in a strained voice. "Irv . . ."

"What's the matter?" Irving asked. "You sick, boss?"

Harvey felt the words bubble inside and then heard them come out. He pointed out the window. "Put a sign on the Essex. Say it's for sale as is. No guarantees. And open up the hood wider. Let 'em take a look at that engine."

Irving gaped at him. "Ya wanna sell it—or ya wanna keep it around for an heirloom? Why, nobody in his right mind would buy that car if they could see what's under the hood."

Harvey sat down heavily in his chair. He felt the perspiration rolling down his face. He opened up the left bottom drawer of the desk and took out a small bottle of whisky, unscrewed the cap, and took a deep gulp. He looked up into Irving's worried face. "What's goin' on?" he asked in a strange, thin voice. "What's the matter with me, Irv? Irv, boobie . . . do I look all right to you?"

Irving's voice was guarded. "What did ya have for dinner?"

Harvey thought for a moment, then made a gesture with his hands, denying any possible gastronomic connection. He set his face, jutted his jaw, let out a laugh dripping with bravado, and reached for the telephone.

"This is nuts," he announced definitely, as he dialed a number. "This is . . . this is power of suggestion or something. That old gleep with the model A! Lemme tell ya, Irv—a real nutsy! Comes in here with this song and dance about a haunted car—"

He heard the receiver lifted at the other end. "Honey," he said into the phone, "it's your ever-lovin'! Listen, baby . . . about tonight . . . yeah, I'm gonna be late. Well, I told ya it was inventory time, didn't I?" He doodled with his free hand, drawing a picture of an old man and a model A Ford. "Of course it's inventory time," he continued, "and what I'm gonna be doin'—" He stopped abruptly. Again his face turned white and again the beads of perspiration came on his forehead and traveled in little rivulets down his face. "As a matter of fact, honey," he heard himself saying, "I'm playin' a little poker with the boys after I close up tonight. And when I told ya last month I was doin' inventory—I was playin' poker then, too!"

At this moment, Harvey thrust the phone away from him as if it were some kind of animal lunging for his throat. He gulped, swallowed, and pulled it to him again.

"Honey," he said in a sick voice, "honey, baby—I think I'm sick or somethin'. What I just told ya . . . well, honey . . . it was a gag . . . what I mean to say is—"

Out came the words again. "I'm gonna play poker with the boys again tonight!" With this, Harvey slammed the phone down and pushed it away. He whirled around to stare at Irving, wild-eyed.

"What's goin' on, Irv? What the hell's the matter with me? I got no control over what I say. I got absolutely no control over—"

Again he stopped, took out his handkerchief and wiped his face. He rose from the chair, went across the room over to the open door, and stared out. There was the model A, sitting all by itself, several feet away from the other cars. Harvey kept staring at it, and finally turned to face Irving.

"Irv," he said, his voice strained, "I'm in the middle of a calamity! That old geezer . . . that gleep I was tellin' ya about . . . he said that car was haunted—and he was right! Ya know what, Irv? Whoever owns that car—*he's got to tell the truth!*"

Harvey clutched at his thick hair, yanking it this way and that. He shook his head back and forth, and his voice was agonized. "Irv, boobie . . . do ya dig it? Can ya think of anything more ghastly?"

He released his hair and pounded himself on the chest. "Me! Harvey Hennicutt! From now on—as long as I own that car—*I gotta keep tellin' the truth!*"

Three days went by. The three longest days that Harvey Hennicutt could ever remember spending. Patsies came and patsies went and Harvey watched them go, quietly wringing his hands or pulling on his hair or just sitting inside his dinky shack, constitutionally unable even to whisper an adjective—let alone make one of his traditional vaunted pitches. Irving, he set to work making signs, and it was a few of these that the assistant brought into the shack and rather forlornly placed around the room. He pointed at them and looked up at Harvey, who sat there, head in hands.

"I finished the signs, boss," he said.

Harvey separated two fingers to let an eyeball free. He nodded perfunctorily, then covered up his face again.

Irving cleared his throat. "You want I should put 'em on the cars . . . or ya wanna read 'em?"

Once again, Harvey peeked through his fingers at the signs. "Not Guaranteed," "In Poor Condition," "Not Recommended," they announced in turn.

Irv shook his head. His voice was disconsolate. "I've heard of low pressure before, boss . . . but I mean, let's face it—this is *no* pressure."

Harvey nodded and let out a small groan. "Irv, boobie," he said in a hospital-ward voice, "do you know that my wife isn't speaking to me? She hasn't spoken to me in three days."

"That ain't your only worry, boss. Do you know that in three days you haven't moved a car off this lot?" He took a step closer to Harvey. "That old lady," he continued, "who came in yesterday afternoon and wanted to buy the old Auburn? Boss—I mean, let's level now! How do ya start a sales pitch by tellin' a customer that if this car was one year older, Moses could've driven it across the Red Sea?" He shook his head. "I mean . . . there's a limit to honesty, boss!"

Harvey nodded his complete approval. "I used to think that, too," he said.

Irv sniffled, changed his weight to the other foot, bit slowly into the end of a cheap cigar, and girded himself for another kind of combat.

"Boss," he said, in a slightly different tone, "I didn't wanna bother ya about this. But . . . well, you know—it's that thing about my raise."

Harvey closed his eyes. "Raise?"

Irv nodded. "It's six months today. I mean . . . I didn't wanna bug ya—but ya promised. You said in six months if I sold three cars—"

Harvey turned in the swivel chair and stared out of the window dreamily, but then his eyes grew wider as he felt another voice rising up within him, just as it had been doing the past three days. He tried to clamp his lips shut and throttle off the oncoming words, but they simply wouldn't be throttled.

"Irving," he heard his voice say, "the day I give you a raise, it'll be below zero on the Fijis!"

The words didn't stop there, though Harvey made a massive, almost inhuman effort to stop them by hurriedly reaching into the bottom desk drawer and pulling out the bottle. But even as he was uncorking it, the rest of the speech spewed out of him like lava out of a volcano.

"Every yokel who's ever worked here starts and stops at the same salary! I just keep dangling a raise in front of 'em for as long as it takes 'em to wise up."

Harvey wanted to say how sorry he was—that he didn't mean it—that he loved Irving like a son—that he certainly *would* get a raise as soon as things got back to normal; but all that came out was a simple sentence.

"For you to get any more dough outta me," Harvey heard himself saying, "would be about as easy as poking hot butter in a wildcat's ear."

Harvey lifted the bottle to his mouth as if it weighed a ton, drank, fought down the nausea, and said—in a strained, quiet voice, "Irving, boobie . . . that hurt me a lot more than it hurt you!"

Irving squared his thin bony shoulders, took a few steps around the desk, stuck a fist into his former master's face.

"Correction," he said firmly, in his high, piping squeal. "This is gonna hurt me a lot worse than it's gonna hurt you."

With that, he swung from the floor, and Harvey watched it coming until it cracked on the point of his jaw. In a portion of his tired, bedraggled mind, he felt surprise that thin little Irving packed such a wallop. He was still carrying this thought as he fell over backward and landed on the floor.

Irving picked up a sign that read, "In Poor Condition—Not Recommended," laid it on Harvey's chest like a funeral wreath, and then stalked righteously out of the room.

Late that night, as Harvey tells it, he sat on the stoop of the shack looking out sadly at his car lot—and particularly at the model A, which stood like some metal pariah staring balefully back at him through its ancient headlights. The banner and bunting flapped noisily in the breeze, mocking him with their sound and with their meaninglessness.

A paunchy gentleman walked briskly into the north end of the lot, stopped, and looked down the line of automobiles. In old and better days, Harvey would've been on his feet and shaking hands and beginning phase one of the attack before the prospective buyer had drawn three breaths. But on this night, Harvey just rose slowly, waved half-heartedly, and leaned against the shack while the man eyed him and walked toward him.

The man in this case was a gentleman named Luther Grimbley. He wore a variation of a frock coat and had small beady eyes. He also wore a cigar in his mouth, which was obviously an accouterment, and he looked as if he had been born with it. He grimly nodded back at Harvey and then looked sideways at the model A. Clearly, this was one of those "thinker"-type buyers who was as anxious to engage in a battle of wills and wiles as Harvey himself. This was quite evident in the rather nonchalant way Mr. Grimbley studied the model A, but kept his eye on Harvey's expression.

Harvey himself, seeing that the man was traditionally an opponent, forced himself to walk over to him. He dredged up some of his old charm, lit his own cigar, tilted his hat an inch farther back on his head, and looked, at this moment, like the Harvey Hennicutt of old.

"What'll be your pleasure tonight?" he asked.

Grimbley kept the cigar in his teeth. "Luther Grimbley, here," he announced, and handed Harvey a card. "Honest Luther Grimbley, thirty years in politics, currently up for reelection—alderman, thirteenth ward. You've probably heard of me."

All of this came out as if it were a single sentence. Harvey took the card and read it.

"Delighted," he said. "Something in a—" He gulped. "A nice model A? It's beautiful, isn't it?"

Then Harvey mentally sat back, waiting for the perverse honesty inside of him to come out with the denial of what he'd just said, but no words came—and for the first time in several days Harvey felt hope rising up inside.

Grimbley removed the cigar, picked off a few errant

fragments of tobacco, and daintily freed them from his fingertips.

"That depends," he said, his eyes half closed. "If you take
twelve aspirin and shut your eyes tight—you might call that
car beautiful. But in the cold light of neon, son—" He
shook his head and pointed to the car. "It's a wreck! What
about its condition?"

Harvey chuckled a deep chuckle and started to retort
with a biblical quote that he usually used in answer to that
question, and one that he had made up himself not six
months before, but he heard himself saying, "The block's
cracked!" He shuddered, clamped tight on the cigar, and half
turned away, damning himself, honesty, the haunted car, and
everything else.

Grimbley's eyebrow rose a little. "Block cracked, you say,
son?"

Harvey nodded tiredly and gave up fighting. "Block
cracked."

"What else?"

Harvey looked down at the tires. "Rubber's almost gone."
He kicked at the tire.

Grimbley went over to the car and also kicked the tire.
"It sure is," he said. Then he made a face and scratched his
jaw. "Might be a few good years left in it." Then, hurriedly,
looking keenly over at Harvey, "Not many, though."

Harvey felt the misery welling up, and also the words.
"Many? *This* car's living on borrowed time!"

Grimbley ran his tongue inside one cheek and drummed
softly on the fender of the model A. He looked at Harvey
squinty-eyed.

"What's she worth?" he asked, and then hurriedly changed
his tone. "I mean, assuming some clod wanted a real bum car
to use for a gag or something."

He chewed off a little piece of the cigar and spit it out, then
walked around the car again. He whistled a continuous low
whistle, sucked in his cheeks, again tapped gently on the
car's fender.

"Maybe fifty bucks?"

Harvey's eyes looked glazed. "Fifty bucks?"

"All right," Grimbley said, "maybe sixty."

"Why not thirty?" Harvey said. "You don't understand, do
you?" He pointed to the car. "It's a bad car. It's a lemon."

Harvey wished fervently at this moment that his tongue
would rot at the roots and he could keep his mouth shut. He

was cursed, damned, and preordained, so he half turned as if ready to walk away and give it up as a bad thing. He was quite unprepared for Grimbley's reaction, for the fat little man stared at him and began to laugh. The laugh turned into a full-throated roar, until it was uncontrollable. Grimbley just stood there and laughed until the tears came out of his eyes.

"Why, you dirty dog, you! Why, you clever son of a—!"

Harvey began to laugh now, too. He didn't know exactly why. Maybe it was release or relief or something—but he joined Grimbley's laughter until his own was a shriek.

"Isn't it the truth?" he screamed. "Isn't it the honest-to-God truth!"

Grimbley wiped his eyes and gradually the laughter died away, though he still shook his head in respectful amazement.

"I've seen all kinds of routines, honest-to-God . . . all kinds of routines." He winked at Harvey and poked him in the chest. "But you clever little cookie, you—this is the old reverse English, isn't it? The old twist-a-roo! Why, you sharp shootin' sharpie!"

He laughed again and clamped the cigar back in his mouth. "You knew I wanted it, didn't you—you little devil, you!" He poked Harvey again. "You knew I wanted it. I'll tell you what," he announced, taking the cigar out, "I'll give you twenty-five bucks for it—mainly on account of it's good politics to drive an old car. Makes people realize you're not getting rich off them!"

He turned to look at the car again. "Make it twenty-two and a half. I didn't notice the dent in the fender." He put the cigar back, squinted his eyes, and looked at Harvey. "Deal?" he asked. "I mean twenty-two fifty, the car—and no strings."

The ecstatic look on Harvey's face slowly dissolved and he felt cold all over. "No strings," he repeated weakly.

Harvey's tone was quite sufficient for Grimbley. Once again his tongue explored the inside of his mouth and he squinted from Harvey to the car and back again.

"You better trot out the strings, buddy boy. Trot out the strings. I want to know what I'm getting!"

Harvey looked off in another direction and closed his eyes. "Twenty-two fifty—the car as is, and . . . and . . ."

"*And what?*"

Harvey turned to him, his voice ghostlike. "It's haunted," he said weakly.

Grimbley took the cigar out of his mouth again and stared at Harvey, and then the laughter came again, uncontrollable, shrieking. "It's haunted!" he shouted. "The goddam car is haunted!" He could barely control himself and just stood there, hands around his vast girth, rolling, wheezing, and half doubled over with hysteria, repeating it over and over again. "It's haunted. The goddam thing is haunted."

Finally he stopped and wiped his eyes, and the cigar was back between his teeth. "So it's haunted! I swear to God, you're the cleverest cookie in fifty states! You ought to be in politics." He laughed again. "It's haunted." He wiped his eyes again, and the chuckle was still in his voice when he asked, "How's it haunted?"

Harvey's eyeballs rolled up in his head. "Whoever owns it," he heard himself say, "has to tell the truth!" There, goddammit, Harvey thought, at least it's out in the air. He could stop worrying about it. The honest Satan inside him had performed the ultimate treachery and forced the admission out.

The word "truth" had a telling effect on Mr. Grimbley. It was as if Harvey had said "smallpox" or "venereal disease" or "the black plague." He let out a long, low breath and took the cigar out of his mouth.

"Has to tell the *truth*?" he asked, pronouncing the word as if it were a profanity.

Harvey nodded. "The whole truth. And the only way you can stop telling the truth is to sell the car."

Again Grimbley gave Harvey his squinty-eyed look and then stared at the model A. He walked a few feet away and pointed to a 1935 Dodge with a rumble seat.

"How about this baby?" he inquired, loading the question with the grape shot of the experienced price-knocker-down.

Harvey heaved a huge sigh. "That's no baby! It's a great grandfather. It's got no transmission, no rear end, no axle. That one's shot."

Immediately after saying this, his shoulders slumped and his normally ruddy face took on the color of an off-white sheet.

Grimbley's eyes sparkled. He was on the precipice of a vast and strange knowledge and he perceived it readily. He took a few steps over to Harvey and spoke in a hushed voice.

"That's the goods, isn't it?" he asked. "You *have* to tell the truth, don't you?" He shook his head from side to side. "That's it! That's the reason for the song and dance. *You have to tell the truth.*"

Harvey smiled the kind of smile that on babies is considered gas. He made a half-hearted gesture toward the car.

"What about the model A?" he said. "Outside of the fact that it's haunted, it's a . . . it's a nice conversation piece."

Grimbley held up a beefy hand. "For some people, maybe," he said positively, "but not for old honest Luther Grimbley! Buddy boy, I'm in politics and when you tell me I gotta start tellin' the truth all the time—" He pulled at his jowls and looked horrified. "Holy God!" He looked back over at the car. "Well, do you know something? I couldn't make a single political speech! I couldn't run for office again. Why, old honest Luther Grimbley . . . old honest Luther Grimbley would die on the vine!"

He carefully butted out the cigar on the sidewalk, scraped off the ashes, and deposited it in his pocket. He started off with a wave of his hand.

"See ya around, buddy boy," he called over his shoulder.

"Hey!" Harvey yelled.

Grimbley stopped and turned to him. Harvey pointed to the car.

"Any suggestions?"

Grimbley looked thoughtful for a moment. "Suggestions? Yeah, maybe one. Why don't ya hang yourself!" Then he turned and walked off.

Harvey leaned against the model A, staring down at his feet, feeling the weight of his depression like sandbags on his shoulders. He took a slow, rather aimless walk over to the shack. He had barely entered the small room when Irving appeared at the door.

He entered silently and picked up a paint brush from a bucket in the corner. He held it up.

"I come back for this."

Harvey nodded numbly and sat down at his desk.

"It belongs to me," Irving said defensively.

Harvey shrugged again and looked at him blankly. "I'm happy for you." He turned in the swivel chair and looked out the window. "I'm like Dante in the inferno," he announced rhetorically. "I'm absolutely like that fella Dante—doomed, damned . . . bankrupt!"

He turned again in the chair to face Irving. "Boobie . . . One man! One clod! One absolute idiot who's got a thing for a pig-in-the-poke! Or one guy whose tellin' the truth all the time might do some good! Irving—is there no such patsy in this city? In this country?"

Irving stared at him, totally without sympathy.

"You're askin' me? You got a helluva nerve! Askin' me about patsies! After I've slaved and worked and broke my back and told lies for ya! You got a helluva nerve even sittin' there talkin' to me! My old man says you're a son of a bitch! And ya know somethin', Hennicutt?"

At this point, Irving slammed his small fist down on the desk. "My old man is right!"

Once again he pounded on the desk for emphasis, and it was then that Harvey noticed the newspaper lying there. He reached over and pulled it to him, turning it so that he could read the headlines. He stared at it for a long moment, then put it down and started to drum his fingers on the desk.

"And, furthermore," Irving's voice squealed, "my old man says that for two cents he'd come over here and give you such a hit in the head you'd never forget it! And, besides that—my sister's husband is goin' to law school at night and I've got every intention of talkin' this whole thing over with him and maybe suing you for contributing to the delinquincy of a minor!"

Harvey's head was bent low over the paper. He gave no sign of hearing Irving's soliloquy, much less being moved by it.

Irving slammed his bony little fist on the desk top again.

"When I think . . . When I think of the terrible things you had me do—like sellin' that 1928 hearse and sayin' it was Babe Ruth's town car!"

He shook his head at the enormity of his past transgressions, but still Harvey Hennicutt kept his eyes fastened on the paper. His lips moved soundlessly as he read something in it, and then, very slowly, he looked up into Irving's face.

"Why not?" he whispered. "I ask ya, Irving, *why not*?"

Irving thrust out a belligerent pointed jaw. "Why not what?"

Harvey slapped the newspaper. "Why not sell it to *him*?"

"Never mind *him*," Irving screeched out. "What about my rights? What about my severance pay? What about my seniority?"

Harvey had the phone book in his hand and was riffling through the pages. He looked up briefly at Irving.

"Irving, boobie . . . I am about to strike a blow for democracy! I don't know *how* I'm goin' to—but I'm goin' to. You and me, boobie," he said, looking down at the phone book. "You and me. This moment is goin' down in history right alongside of Washington crossing the Delaware, the invasion of Normandy, and the repeal of the Eighteenth Amendment!"

Irving gaped at him. "What?" he inquired in a soft voice.

"Exactly!" Harvey said. *"And you are there!"*

He grabbed the phone and pulled it toward him. He started to dial a number, and at the same time looked up at Irving.

"You run out and dust off that Packard—the one with the sawdust in the wheel bearings."

"Check, boss," Irving said, as he turned smartly and headed for the door.

Harvey Hennicutt was functioning again. Irving could hear the great man's voice on the telephone. It rang with some of the old assurance, the verve, and the grandeur of the man who had once actually sold a Mack truck to a midget along with a written guarantee that the midget would grow an inch and a quarter each year just by stretching to reach the pedals.

It was eight in the morning when a long, sleek black limousine pulled into Harvey Hennicutt's used-car lot. Harvey, hearing it stop, left the shack and went over to it. He noticed immediately that it was driven by a chauffeur who had a build like Mickey Hargitay.

There was a huddled figure in the back seat who sat motionless with his coat collar hiding his face, but the front door opened and out stepped a dapper little man with a face like a chicken hawk. He gave Harvey a no-nonsense nod, looked around at the various cars, with a raised eyebrow, then pointed to the model A.

"This is the car, I presume?"

Harvey nodded. "That's the baby."

"Baby?"

"It's an American expression," Harvey explained. "We call everything 'baby.' "

He looked over the little man's shoulder at the black limousine. "That's not a bad-lookin' baby *you're* drivin'. You're not thinkin' of trading that in, are you?"

The little man shook his head decisively. "I am interested only in this so-called model A you described on the telephone."

Harvey smiled at him. Then he winked, and jammed an elbow into the little man's rib cage.

"Got to ya, didn't I?"

He jerked a thumb in the direction of the model A.

"Wouldn't that be a blast. You take that car back to your country, tell 'em that this is a sample of what the capitalists drive?" Again he rammed an elbow into the little man's side. "That's worth six points, ain't it?"

The little man dusted off his coat, moved a step back, and surveyed Harvey, half with horror and half with a curious, clinical interest.

"Precisely what we choose to do with the automobile," he said tersely, "is *our* business, so long as we agree on the terms. You said that the automobile was three hundred dollars?"

Harvey noted that the little man was already reaching into his coat for a wallet.

"Three hundred dollars," Harvey explained hurriedly, "is for the car without the extras."

He felt his eyeballs swell as the little man dug into the wallet and started to extract bills.

"The hub caps are extra—that's twenty bucks. The hand crank—not that you'll probably need it—that I'll practically give away for twelve."

His practiced eye was a gimlet microscope as he looked over at the model A.

"That special window glass—" He felt the truth rising up in him and heard himself say at this point, "It ain't unbreakable, I mean."

"Not unbreakable?" the little man inquired.

"It breaks, is what I mean," Harvey explained, and then deciding that discretion was the better part of valor, he wordlessly pulled out several papers, spread them out on the hood of an incredibly aged Jordan 8.

"Now if you'll just sign there," Harvey said, whipping out a pen. "That's the transfer of ownership, title, and memorandum of sale. Each one is in triplicate and I put an X where you gotta sign each one."

The little man collected the papers and carried them over to the black limousine. He tapped on the rear window and a large, pudgy hand came out to take the papers. It disappeared with them into the dark confines of the rear seat. There was a muffled inquiry in a strange language. The little man turned, called out to Harvey.

"My—my 'employer' would like to know if a guarantee comes with this automobile."

Again, Harvey had that ice-cold feeling. It had come—that moment of truth again. He smiled weakly. Coughed. Blew his nose. Hummed a short selection from "Guys and Dolls."

Looked wildly over his shoulder to see if he could find Irving and change the subject. But the question hung over him like Damocles' sword, and all of his ritual, he knew very well, was simply a delaying rear-guard action. He had to make his stand—and make it he did.

"The car's haunted," he said, in a hollow, muffled voice.

The little man looked at him with a raised eyebrow. "Haunted?" he inquired.

Harvey unloaded his caution in one fell swoop. "Haunted it is," he said. "Real haunted. I mean, it's like . . . it's like *haunted*! And that's somethin' you can't say about any other car you've ever seen!"

Harvey's voice went on, buoyed up by truth, propelled out by honesty, and given a lyrical quality by his sheer desperation.

"Lemme tell ya somethin', buddy," he said, walking over to the little man to poke him with a forefinger. "A lot of these cars are real gone. I mean *long* gone. And some of 'em are absolute first-rate bonafide lemons. I got some I keep behind the shack, camouflaged, because they're the old busteroo's!"

He whirled around and pointed dramatically toward the model A. "But that car—that model . A— That car is absolutely haunted. I guarantee it. *It is like absolutely haunted!*"

The interpreter, or whoever he was, turned and said a few words into the back seat of the car, and, after a moment, was handed some papers by the person sitting there. He passed these over to Harvey.

"Here you are," he said. "All signed." He looked at the model A over Harvey's shoulder. "Now, I presume the car has petrol?" he inquired.

"Petrol?" Harvey made a face. "You mean like—like—"

"Gasoline," the little man interrupted. "Does it have a full tank of gasoline?"

"She's loaded up," Harvey said. "You can just drive 'er away, buddy."

The little man nodded, satisfied, motioned to the chauffeur, who got out of the limousine. Harvey turned, kicked his heels together in the air, and then waltzed back over to the shack like some ponderous ballet dancer. He took the four steps in one leap, slammed his way into the room, grabbed Irving by the ears, and planted a big wet kiss on his forehead. He held out the papers, and studied them. For the first time in days he felt an incredible lightness of mind and body, as if he had just been removed from a concrete cast.

Irving was both frightened and impressed as he looked out through the open door at the black limousine departing.

"You know what that is, boss? That's what they call a Zis. It's Russian."

Harvey kicked over a wastebasket with sheer animal joy. "That's what she is," he said. "Irving, boobie," he gushed, as he leaped up on the desk, upsetting an inkwell and a basket of papers, "this is very likely the happiest day of my life!"

Irving was not listening to him any more. He was staring, wide-eyed, out the door as the model A chugged past him.

"Boss," Irving whispered, "boss, you sold it!"

He turned to stare at Harvey, then slowly his eyes lowered to the newspaper, still on the desk. The headline read, "Khrushchev visiting UN."

"Khrushchev." Irving barely got it out. "Nikita Khrushchev."

He took a hesitant step toward the desk, where Harvey stood like some off-beat god in a pool of ink and torn papers. Irving looked up at him with awe and reverence.

"That's who you sold the car to, wasn't it, boss? Nikita Khrushchev."

Harvey held out the registration papers in his hand and pointed to a signature. "Irving, boobie," he announced senatorially, "from this second on, when that old lard-head starts to walk on his lower lip—it comes out like the truth!"

"Boss," Irving whispered, feeling himself in the presence of some kind of diety, "boss . . . how the hell did ya do it?"

Harvey lowered the papers and placed them on the desk well away from the pool of ink. He thought for a moment and then spoke.

"Acumen, Irving," he finally said, in a gentle voice. "Stick-to-itiveness. Will. Determination. Perseverance. Patriotism. Unselfishness. Resolve." He lit a cigar. "And also the fact that if I had to tell the truth one more time, I'd've had to commit suicide!"

He took the cigar out of his mouth and surveyed it at arm's length. "Know what I told 'em, Irv? I told 'em it'd be a real blast to take the raunchiest-lookin' puddle jumper ever to come out of Detroit, take it back to the USSR and put it on display. Propaganda! That was the pitch. Show all of them walking Muscovites just what the average American drives —or at least what Nikita would like 'em to *believe* we drive."

Irving's face looked drawn and his eyes narrowed slightly. "Boss," he said, "that ain't patriotic."

Harvey beamed at him from his Mount Olympus of righteousness and holy zeal.

"Irving," he said patiently, "that's what I *told* 'em they could do with the car, but that isn't what they're gonna be *able* to do with it. When Fatty starts that kind of pitch, it isn't gonna come out that way."

He chuckled softly, got down off the desk, reached for the phone, studied it a moment, then started to dial a number.

"Irving," he said, over his shoulder to the boy standing there like a pilgrim seeing a miracle performed. "Irving, run out there and close the hood on the Essex—and if anybody should come within ten feet of it, you lasso 'em. Tell 'em that that car was formerly owned by a lady embalmer who won it at a raffle at a DAR convention in Boston, but it was only used once a year as a float on Fourth of July parades."

Irving's eyes shone with almost tearful respect and admiration.

"Right, boss," he choked. "I'll attend to it."

He turned and went outside, as Harvey heard the operator's voice on the phone.

"Yes, ma'am," he said, chewing on the cigar. "I think I'll probably need Information. . . . That's correct. . . . Ya see, what I had in mind was that if an American citizen had somethin' real important in the way of news . . . I mean . . . if it affected the policy of the United States . . . what I mean is —if from now on, everything that fat boy over there said was the absolute truth—well, what I'd really like to know is . . . *Can you get me through to Jack Kennedy?*"

Then he sat back, chewing happily on his cigar, as outside the noise of Irving's pounding down the hood of the aged Essex came over the quiet lot like a clarion call to arms.

Harvey Hennicutt, as he tells it, was eminently satisfied.

THE
SHELTER

OUTSIDE it was a summer night. Broad-leaved oaks and maples caught the lights of the old stately houses that flanked the street. A breeze carried with it the eight o'clock noises of television westerns, kids asking for glasses of water, and the discordant tinkle of a piano.

In Dr. Stockton's house, the meal had been eaten, and his wife, Grace, was bringing in the birthday cake. The people at the table rose, applauded, whistled—and somebody began singing "Happy Birthday to You," and then they all joined in.

Bill Stockton blushed, put his head down, held up his hand in protest, but down deep he felt incredibly happy.

Marty Weiss, a small, dark, intense little guy who ran a shoe store on Court Street, got to his feet and shouted out:

"Speech, Doc. Let's have a speech!"

Bill Stockton blushed again. "Lay off me, will ya—you crazy people. A surprise party is all my heart can take. You want to lose your friendly family physician?"

There was laughter, and then Jerry Harlowe—a big, tall man, who had gone to college with Bill—stood up and held out his glass.

"Before he blows out the candles," Harlowe announced pontifically, "I should like to propose a toast, since no birthday celebration is complete without a traditional after-dinner address."

Martha Harlowe gave him a Bronx cheer and Marty's wife, Rebecca, tried to pull him down by the back of his coat. Harlowe leaned over and gave her a big wet kiss and they all shrieked with laughter. Then he held up his glass again, waved off Grace's protest that first her husband should blow out the candles, and addressed the group.

"And now to get down to the business at hand—that of honoring one Dr. William Stockton, who's grown one year older and who will admit to being over twenty-one."

Again they all laughed, and Grace leaned over to hug her husband.

Harlowe turned toward Bill Stockton and smiled, and there was something in the smile that made them all become quiet.

"We got this little surprise party together, Bill," he said, "as a very small reminder to you that on this particular street, and in this particular town, you're a very beloved guy. There isn't one of us in this room who hasn't put in a frantic phone call to you in the middle of the night with a sick kid or a major medical crisis that turns out to be indigestion. And you'd come out with that antique medical bag of yours, one eye closed and half asleep, but without even a moment's hesitation. And while things like this never appear on a bill under 'services rendered,' you made a lot of hearts beat easier, and you've eased more pain than I'd ever like to feel."

He grinned, then winked at the people who were listening so intently.

"And there also isn't one of us in this room," he continued, "who hasn't owed you a whopping bill for a lot of months, and I expect there are plenty of us on this street who owe you one now."

There was laughter at this. And Marty Weiss banged on his glass with a fork.

"What about his hammering at all hours of the night?" he called out. "That's another thing we owe him for."

Jerry Harlowe joined in the laughter, then held up his hands.

"Oh, yes," he said, with a smile. "The good doctor's bomb shelter. I think we might as well forgive him for that, despite the fact that what he thinks is far-sightedness on his part is a pain in the neck to all the rest of us on this street. The concrete trucks, the nocturnal hammering, and all the rest of it."

They all laughed again, and Bill Stockton looked around quizzically, knife in hand.

"I can tell you all this," he said. "You don't get any cake until the windbag is finished."

"Why, Bill Stockton!" his wife said, with gentle admonition.

"Bill's right," Marty interjected. "Go ahead, Jerry, get it over with while we're still sober enough to eat."

Harlowe picked up his wine glass again. "This is the end right here. When Grace mentioned that it was your birthday, we took it on ourselves to handle the proceedings. And just as a little personal aside, let me conclude this way. A toast to Dr. William Stockton, whom I've known for better than twenty years. To all the nice things he's done for a lot of people—and because he's forty-four years old, and because we wish him a minimum forty-four more to keep being the same kind of guy he is, and the way he always has been. Happy birthday, you old bastard."

He took a long swig and Rebecca Weiss suddenly began to cry.

"Oh, my dear God," announced Marty. "Down goes a speech, up comes my wife's tears."

Bill Stockton blew out the candles, then looked up with a mock sardonic look. "I don't blame her," he said. "First a surprise party—and I abhor surprise parties—and then a sloppy sentimental speech." He turned toward Harlowe and held out his hand. "But just between you and me and the American Medical Association—you're nice people to have around, whether you pay your bills or not."

He turned and looked down the length of the table, and held up his own glass. "May I reciprocate, my friends. To my neighbors—with my thanks that you're in the neighborhood."

"Amen," whispered Marty Weiss, and turned to his wife. "And if you cry again, I'll belt you." He leaned over and kissed her, and Bill Stockton started to cut the cake.

"Hey, pop."

It was Stockton's son, Paul, who came into the dining room. He was a twelve-year-old mass of freckles and looked like a pint-size version of the doctor.

"The television set just went out."

Stockton held out his hands in dismay. "Gad, crisis, crisis, crisis! And how can the world survive without the 'Untouchables' and 'Huckleberry Hound'?"

"It was the 'U.S. Steel Hour,'" the boy said seriously. "And the picture went out and then there was some kind of crazy announcement. Something about . . ."

He continued to speak, but he was drowned out by Martha Harlowe laughing at something Rebecca had said to her. But Marty Weiss, closest to the boy, suddenly looked serious. He got out of his seat and turned to the others.

"Hold it, everybody," he said tensely. Then he turned toward Paul. "What did you say, Paul?"

"The announcer said something about turning to the Conelrad station on the radio. What's that mean? Hasn't that got something to do with—"

He stopped abruptly. There was a sudden absolute stillness.

"You must have heard it wrong, Paul," his father said quietly.

The boy shook his head. "I didn't hear it wrong, pop. That's what he said. To turn on your Conelrad station. Then everything went blank."

A gasp came from Jerry Harlowe. A woman let out a cry. They ran into the living room behind Stockton, who immediately turned the knob on a small table-model radio, and stared down at it grimly. After a moment, there came the voice of an announcer. . . .

"Direct from Washington, D.C. Repeating that. Four minutes ago, the President of the United States made the following announcement—I quote: 'At eleven-O-four P.M. Eastern Standard Time, both our Distant Early Warning and Ballistics Early Warning line reported radar evidence of unidentified flying objects, flying on a course due southeast. As of this moment, we have been unable to determine the nature of these objects, but for the time being, in the interest of national safety, we are declaring a state of Yellow Alert.' "

There was a moment's silence, and Grace seized the doctor's arm. With her free hand, she reached for Paul and drew him to her.

Rebecca Weiss started to cry, and her husband, Marty, just stood there, his face white.

The voice on the radio continued:

"The Civil Defense authorities request that if you have a shelter already prepared, go there at once. If you do not have a shelter, use your time to move supplies, food, water, and medicine to a central place. Keep all windows and doors closed. We repeat: If you're in your home, go to your prepared shelters or to your basement. . . ."

The voice of the announcer continued, went on and on, repeating the unbelievable introduction to an incredible horror.

They all stood gaping at the radio, and in one fragment of a moment they thought:

The baby, Rebecca Weiss thought. The tiny baby asleep in their house across the street. Four months old. And they had kidded about it this morning. Marty had said they should send her to Vassar, and she'd chuckled about it all morning. Send the baby to Vassar. And suddenly, in searing agony, it occurred to her, that they would have no baby. This infant thing they had built their lives around—she would cease to exist.

I don't believe it, Marty thought. He shook his head. He rejected it. It simply wasn't happening. It was a magazine story or a movie. It was some idle chatter at a party. It was a pamphlet that some kook had left on a doorstep, but it wasn't happening—it couldn't be happening . . . but all the time he knew it was. It was true. It was happening.

I want to cry, thought Jerry Harlowe, I want to cry. I can feel the tears inside me. But I mustn't cry—I'm a man. But the claims . . . the insurance claims. My God—they'd be enormous! He could go bankrupt! It was like a joke. A cold, formless joke. Humor in an insane asylum. A crazy accountant trying to add up an earthquake. Sure—he'd go bankrupt. The world would turn into a jungle. And he'd go bankrupt.

The roses, Jerry's wife, Martha, thought suddenly. The beautiful American Beauties that she'd so lovingly and painstakingly cared for—and this year they had come up so wonderfully. They were so beautiful. Then she clenched her fists and let her fingernails dig into the flesh of her palms, hating herself for the thought. What about the children? What about Ann and Charley? How, in God's name, could a mother think about a rose garden at this moment when death had just been announced over the radio? She shut her eyes tightly, wishing it all away—but when she opened them, the room was there and all the people in it. She felt a sudden nausea rising up inside her—a wave of sickness that left her weak and perspiring.

The pain, Dr. Stockton thought. The incredible pain. He could remember reading about Hiroshima. The burn cases. The radiation poisoning. The scarred, agonized flesh that sent a protracted scream over the dying city. He remembered it was something the Japanese doctors could not cope with. It had been too sudden, too unexpected, agony on a mass scale. This thing that hovered over them now, was whole streets and cities and states; millions and millions of people suddenly thrust into a malestrom—a slaughterhouse on a scale that couldn't even be measured by the holocaust that was Hiroshima.

So each stood there with a secret thought, while the voice of the radio announcer, quivering with a barely perceptible tension, kept on repeating the announcements over and over again in the same studiedly dispassionate voice—the well-rehearsed ritual of a modern Paul Revere on a twentieth-century night-ride. One if by land or two if by sea, but there was no opposite shore. They were all in this together. There was no escape. There was no defense. Death was en route to them over the Alaskan snow, and all anyone could do was simply to announce its coming.

They ran out of the Stockton house, frantic, panicky—with vague plans for survival propelling them to their own houses. But then a siren rang out—its eerie shriek piercing the summer night, pinioning their thoughts in the night's darkness and holding them in fear-frozen suspension until once again they could break loose and race toward their homes.

And, in each of them, as they ran frantically across the street and down sidewalks and across lawns, was one single awareness. The street was somehow different. It had no familiarity. It was as if each of them had been away for a hundred years and suddenly returned. It was a vast place of strangeness.

And the siren continued to scream its discordant wail through the summer night.

Bill Stockton had placed the radio in the kitchen where Grace was filling water jugs.

"This is Conelrad, your emergency broadcasting station. You will find Conelrad at either six forty or twelve forty on your dial. Remain tuned to this frequency. We repeat our previous announcement. We are in a state of Yellow Alert. If you have a shelter already prepared, go there at once. If you do not have a shelter, use your time to move supplies of food, water, and medicine to a central place. Keep all windows and doors closed. We repeat: If you're in your home, go to your prepared shelters or to your basement. . . ."

The water dribbled out of the faucet, the pressure growing weaker each moment.

Paul hurried through the kitchen, carrying a box of canned goods, and went down the cellar steps.

Bill Stockton came into the kitchen after him, and picked up two of the filled jugs of water on the floor.

"Fill up as many as you can, Grace," he said tersely. "I'm going to start the generator up in the shelter in case the power goes off."

He looked toward the fluorescent light over the sink. Already it was beginning to dim. Stockton looked grim.

"That may happen any moment," he said.

"There's hardly any water coming through the tap," Grace said, a catch in her voice.

"That's because everybody and his brother is doing the same thing we are. Keep it on full force until it stops." He turned toward the basement door.

"Here," Grace called out after him. "Take this one with you. It's filled."

She started to remove the heavy jug from the sink. It slipped out of her hand and fell, smashing to the floor and sending glass cascading around the room.

Grace let out one sob and shoved a fist into her mouth to hold back any more. For just one moment she felt herself falling into hysteria, wanting to scream, wanting to run frantically somewhere, anywhere, wanting unconsciousness to release her from the nightmare that was going on inside her kitchen.

Bill Stockton took hold of her and held her tight. His voice was gentle, but it didn't sound like his voice at all.

"Easy, honey—easy." He pointed to the broken jug. "Make believe it's perfume and it cost a hundred bucks an ounce." He stared down at the bottle of water at his feet. "Maybe in an hour," he said thoughtfully, "it'll be worth more than that."

Paul came up from the basement.

"What else, pop?"

"All the canned goods down?"

"All that I could find."

"How about the fruit cellar?" Grace asked him, keeping her voice steady.

"I put all those in, too," Paul responded.

"Get my bag from the bedroom," Stockton said. "Put that down there, too."

"What about books and stuff?" Paul said.

When Grace spoke her voice broke and the words came out tight and loud—louder than her son could ever remember, and different, too.

"Dammit! Your father told you to get his bag—!"

The boy let out an incredulous gasp. It was his mother, but it wasn't his mother. The voice wasn't hers. The expression wasn't hers. He gave a frightened sob.

"That's all right," Stockton said softly, pushing the boy out. "We're just frightened, Paul. We're not ourselves. Go ahead, son."

Then he turned to his wife. "We'll need books, Grace. God knows how long we'll have to stay down there." Then, in a gentle tone, almost supplicating, "Honey, try to get hold of yourself. It's the most important thing on God's earth now."

He watched her for a moment, then very deliberately turned to look toward the cupboards to the left of the sink.

"What about light bulbs?" he asked. "Where do you keep the light bulbs?"

Grace pointed. "Top shelf in that cupboard there." Then she bit her lip. "We don't have any. I ran out yesterday. I was going to buy some at the store. There was a sale on—"

She leaned against the sink and felt the tears running down her face. "Oh, my God!" she said. "I'm talking like an idiot. A sale at the store. Oh, God in heaven! The world is about to explode and I'm talking about a sale at the store!"

Stockton reached out and touched her face.

"It doesn't make any difference," he said to her quietly. "You can mouth all the idiocies you want to. Just don't panic, Grace. That's the most important thing now." He held her hand tightly. *"We mustn't panic."*

"How much time do we have?"

"There's no telling. I think I remember reading some place that from the first alarm, we might have anywhere from fifteen minutes to a half an hour."

Grace's eyes grew large. "Fifteen minutes?"

He shook his head. "I'm guessing, Grace. I don't know for sure. I don't think anyone does."

He went into the dining room. "Keep getting the water," he said to her over his shoulder.

Paul came down the steps through the front hall and into the living room. He carried an armful of books and magazines, and on top of them his father's medical bag.

"I got everything, pop."

"Let me give you a hand," said Stockton, taking the things out of his arms.

Paul turned, and started toward the front door.

"Paul!" Stockton shouted at him. "Are you out of your mind? Stay inside here."

"My bike's outside," the boy said.

"You won't need it. Go on down to the shelter."

"But if they do drop a bomb or something, it'll burn everything up. I know, pop. I read it. If it's a hydrogen bomb, there won't be anything left standing."

Stockton let the magazines drop to the floor. He walked over to his son and gripped him by the shoulders. There was a fierceness to his voice.

"Don't even think that! Don't let yourself think that—and don't say anything about it in front of your mother. She's counting on us, Paul. We're the men here."

He released the boy with one last gentle squeeze.

"As a matter of fact . . . as a matter of fact, we may be out of the danger zone. We might be two or three hundred miles from where the bomb drops. We may not even *know* that it's dropped—"

"Pop," Paul interrupted. "We're forty miles from New York. If they dropped a hydrogen bomb . . ." He looked into his father's eyes. "We'll know it all right, pop."

Stockton stared at this replica of himself, filled with love and pride.

"If we do, Paul," he said quietly, "then we do, that's all —but for the time being our job is to stay alive, and you're not going to stay alive running out in the night trying to find a bicycle."

Grace's voice came from the kitchen, shaky and high. "Bill?" She appeared at the dining-room door. "Bill, there's no more water."

"It doesn't make any difference," Stockton said. "I think we've got enough now anyway. Bring a jug with you, Grace. Paul and I will come back up for the rest of it."

They carried the jugs and the rest of the things down the basement steps and through the door of the shelter, which was at the far end of the cellar.

Grace put down the jug and looked around the small room. Bunk beds, can-ladened shelves, the generator, stacks of books and magazines, medical supplies. Suddenly their whole existence had telescoped into this tiny place loaded with things that up to half an hour ago had had no great significance. Half an hour ago! Grace suddenly recollected that in thirty minutes everything on earth had turned upside down. Every value, every belief, every frame of reference, had suddenly ceased to exist or had taken on a vast life-or-death importance. She watched her husband and Paul leave the shelter and start up the steps toward the kitchen.

Stockton stopped halfway up.

"I forgot," he said. "There's a five-gallon can of gasoline in the garage. Paul, you run out and get that. We'll need it for the generator."

"Right, pop."

Stockton looked briefly across to the cellar toward the open door of the shelter. Grace sat on one of the bunk beds staring at nothing. He hesitated a moment, then hurried up to the kitchen, picked up two of the three remaining jugs of water, and went downstairs again.

Grace looked up as he entered the shelter. Her voice was a

whisper. "Bill . . . Bill, this is so incredible. We must be dreaming. It can't really be happening."

Stockton knelt down in front of her and took both her hands.

"I just told Paul," he said to her, "if it's a bomb, there's no certainty that it'll land near us. And if it doesn't—"

Grace pulled her hands away.

"But if it does," she said. "If it hits New York, we'll get it, too. All of it. The poison, the radiation—we'll get it, too."

"We'll be in the shelter, Grace," Stockton said, "and with any luck at all, we'll survive. We've got enough food and water to last us at least two weeks . . . maybe even longer, if we use it wisely."

Grace looked at him blankly. "And then what?" she asked, in a still voice. "Then what, Bill? We crawl out of here like gophers to tiptoe through all the rubble up above. The rubble and the ruins and the bodies of our friends . . ."

She stopped, and stared down at the floor. When she looked up at him again, there was a different expression on her face—deeper than panic, more enveloping than fear—resignation, abject surrender.

"Why is it so necessary that we survive?" she asked in a flat voice. "What's the good of it, Bill?—wouldn't it be quicker and easier if we just . . ." She let the word dangle.

Paul's voice called, "I got the gasoline, pop. Is that all you need from out here?"

"Bring the can, Paul," his father said. Then he turned to Grace. For the first time there was a tremor in his voice.

"That's why we have to survive," he said. "That's the reason."

They heard Paul's steps.

"He may inherit just rubble, but he's twelve years old. It isn't just our survival, Grace. Sure, we can throw our lives away. Just deposit them on the curb like garbage cans." His voice went higher. *"He's twelve years old.* It's too goddam early to think about a boy dying . . . when he hasn't even had a chance to do any living."

Paul appeared at the door with the gasoline can.

"Put it there, next to the generator," Stockton said as he walked out of the room. "I'll go up and get the rest of the water."

He climbed back up the stairs to the kitchen and picked up the last of the jugs. He was about to carry it back down when he heard a knock on the kitchen door. Jerry Harlowe's face peered through the parted curtains.

Stockton unlocked the door. Harlowe stood outside, with a smile on his face that looked as if it had been painted on. His voice was strained.

"How ya doin', Bill?" he asked.

"I'm collecting water, which is what you should be doing."

Harlowe looked painfully ill at ease.

"We got about thirty gallons and then the water stopped," he said. His face twisted again. "Did yours stop too, Bill?"

Stockton nodded. "You better get on home, Jerry. Get into your shel—" He wet his lips and corrected himself. "Into your basement. I'd board up the windows if I were you, and if you've got any wood putty or anything, I'd seal the corners."

Harlowe fiddled with his tie.

"We don't have a cellar, Bill," he said, with a lopsided grin. "Remember? The benefits of modern architecture. We've got the one brand-new house on the street. Everything at your beck and call. Everything at your fingertips—" His voice shook. "Every wonder of modern science taken into account . . . except the one they forgot." He put his eyes down and stared at his feet. "The one that's heading for us now."

He looked up slowly and swallowed. "Bill," he said, in a whisper, "can I bring Martha and the kids over here?"

Stockton froze. He felt anger. "Over here?"

Harlowe nodded eagerly. "We're sitting ducks there. Sitting ducks. We don't have any protection at all."

Stockton thought for a moment, then turned away. "You can use our basement."

Harlowe grabbed his arm. "Your basement?" he asked incredulously. "What about your shelter? Goddammit, Bill, that's the only place anybody can survive. We've got to get into a shelter!"

Stockton looked at him, and the anger that had been just a dull resentment surged up inside. He held it down with effort, wondering to himself how the familiar face, once pleasing and boyish, could be so abhorrent to him now.

"I don't have any room, Jerry," he said. "I don't have nearly enough room—or supplies, or anything. It's designed for three people."

"We'll bring our own water," Harlowe said, eagerly, "and our own food. We'll sleep on top of one another if necessary." His voice broke. "Please, Bill . . ."

He stared at Stockton's impassive face. "Bill, we've got to use your shelter!" he cried. "I've got to keep my family alive! And we won't use any of your stuff. Don't you understand? We'll bring our own."

Stockton looked down at Harlowe's hands, then into his face.

"What about your own air? Will you bring your own air? That's a ten-by-ten room, Jerry."

Harlowe let his hands drop. "Just let us stay in there the first forty-eight hours or so. Then we'll get out. Honest to God, Bill. No matter what, we'll get out."

Stockton felt the water jug heavy in his hand. This could not be prolonged, he knew that. His voice cut through the air like a scalpel.

"When that door gets closed, Jerry, it stays closed. Closed and locked. There'll be radiation—and God knows what else." He felt an anguish rising deep inside him. "I'm sorry, Jerry. As God is my witness—I'm sorry. But I built that for *my* family."

He turned and started for the basement.

Jerry's voice followed him. "What about *mine*? What do *we* do? Just rock on the front porch until we get burned to cinders!"

Stockton kept his back to him. "That's not my concern. Right at this moment, it's my family I have to worry about."

He started down the steps. Harlowe ran after him and grabbed his arm.

"I'm not going to sit by and watch my wife and my kids die in agony!" Tears rolled down Harlowe's face. "Do you understand, Bill? I'm not going to do that!"

He shook Stockton, and started to cry uncontrollably. "I'm not going to—"

Stockton pulled away. The jug slipped out of his hand and bounced down the basement steps, but it did not break. Stockton went slowly down the steps and picked it up.

"I'm sorry," he heard Harlowe say. "Please forgive me, Bill."

Stockton turned to look up. Oh, God, he thought. That's my friend standing there. That's my friend. But then his anger returned. He spoke to the figure standing above him.

"I kept telling you—all of you. Build a shelter. Get ready. Forget the card parties and the barbeques for maybe a couple of hours a week and admit to yourself that the worst is possible."

He shook his head. "But you didn't want to listen, Jerry. None of you wanted to listen. To build a shelter was admitting the kind of age we're living in—and none of you had the guts to make that kind of an admission."

He closed his eyes for a moment and then took a deep breath. "So now, Jerry, now you've got to face the reality."

He took one last look at the white, stricken face on the stairs. "You want help now, Jerry? Now you get it from God." He shook his head. "Not from me."

He walked across the cellar toward the shelter.

The front door opened and the Weisses hurried through the hall into the living room. Rebecca carried their baby in her arms and stayed close to Marty.

"Bill!" Marty called. "Bill—where are you?"

"They're already in the shelter!" Rebecca cried hysterically. "I told you they'd be in the shelter! They've locked themselves in."

Jerry Harlowe appeared from the kitchen. "It's no use," he said. "He won't let anyone in."

Marty's dark little face twisted with fear. "He's *got* to let us in!" He pointed toward Rebecca and the baby. "We don't even have any windows in half the basement. I don't have anything to plug them up with either."

He started to push his way past Harlowe. "Where is he? Is he downstairs? Is he in the shelter?"

He walked through the dining room into the kitchen, saw the open basement door, and called down.

"Bill? Bill—it's Marty. We've got the baby with us."

He stumbled down the cellar steps, calling, "Bill? Bill?"

The lights dimmed in the basement and Marty groped his way across the cellar floor until he reached the metal door of the shelter, now closed.

Behind him, in the darkness, his wife's voice called out.

"Marty! Marty—where are you? The lights are out! Marty —please . . . come back and get us."

The baby started to cry, and then, from outside, came the sound of the siren.

Marty pounded on the door of the shelter. "Bill! Please . . . Bill . . . let us in!"

Stockton's voice came back, muffled, from the other side of the door.

"Marty, I would if I could. Do you understand? If it didn't mean endangering the lives of my own family, I would. I swear to you, I would."

The last part of his words were drowned out by the siren, and then by the shrill wailing of the baby from the steps. Panic clawed at Marty and he pounded on the door with both hands.

"Bill!" he shouted. *"You've got to let us in!* There isn't any time. Please, Bill!"

On the other side of the door, the generator had begun to hum and the lights went on in the shelter—two big one-hundred watt bulbs, glaringly white.

Bill Stockton put his head against the steel door and closed his eyes. He shook his head.

"I can't, Marty. Don't stay there asking me. I can't."

His mouth went tight and his voice shook. "I can't and I won't!"

Marty Weiss knew then that the door was to remain locked. He turned and peered through the darkness at the figure of his wife standing on the steps. He felt a surge of tenderness. Of love. And, at this moment—of a loss, final and irrevocable. He turned and stared at the closed door.

"I feel sorry for you, Bill," he said, quietly but clearly. "I really do. You'll survive. You'll live through it." His voice went higher. "But you're going to have blood on your hands. Do you hear me, Bill? You'll have blood on your hands."

Inside the shelter, Stockton stared at his wife. She tried to say something to him, but nothing came out.

Stockton could hear Marty Weiss's footsteps retreating through the cellar and up the steps. His hands shook, and he had to clasp them together to keep them still.

"I can't help it," he whispered. "It's us or it's them. All my life . . . all my life I've only had one function. That was to end suffering. Relieve pain. To cure. But the rules are different now. The rules, the time, the place. Now there's only one purpose, Grace—that's to survive. Nothing else means anything. And we can't afford to *let* it mean anything." Suddenly he whirled to the door. "Marty! Jerry!" he screamed. "All of you—any of you! Get out of here! *Stay* out of here!"

Behind him he could hear his son beginning to cry.

"God damn it! God damn it! If there's blood on my hands . . . all of you—all of you put it there!"

And then he began to tremble. Fatigue struck him like a blow; he felt as if he could no longer stand up, and he sat down on one of the cots.

Far off there was the sound of the siren.

Bill Stockton closed his eyes tightly and tried to make his mind go blank. But the sound persisted, and he felt a massive pain.

A group of neighbors collected outside Bill Stockton's house. One of them carried a portable radio, and the voice of the Conelrad announcer supplied an urgent background to the whispered questions and the occasional cry of a child or a woman.

Harlowe came out from the house and stood on the front porch. Marty Weiss and his wife followed him.

Martha Harlowe pushed her way through the group, holding tight to the hands of her children. "Jerry," she called toward the porch, "what happened?"

Harlowe shook his head. "Nothing happened. I think we all better go back and try to fix up the cellars."

"That's crazy!" a man's voice said. "There's no time for that. Bill's got the only place on the street that would do any good."

A woman cried out, "It'll land any minute!" Her voice was frantic. "I know it—it's going to land any minute!"

"This is Conelrad," the radio announced. "This is Conelrad. We are still in a state of Yellow Alert. If you are a public official or a government employee with an emergency assignment, or a Civil Defense worker, you should report to your post immediately. If you are a public official or government employee . . ." The voice continued underneath the flood of voices.

A big, burly man who lived on the corner started up the steps to Stockton's porch. Jerry Harlowe stood in his way.

"Don't waste your time," Harlowe said. "He won't let anyone in."

The man turned helplessly toward his wife, who stood at the foot of the steps.

"What'll we do?" the woman asked, panic building in her voice. "What are we going to do?"

"Maybe we ought to pick out just one basement," Marty Weiss said, "and go to work on it. Pool all our stuff. Food, water—everything."

"It isn't fair," Martha Harlowe said. She pointed toward the Stockton porch. "He's down there in a bomb shelter —completely safe. And *our* kids have to just wait around for a bomb to drop!"

Her nine-year-old daughter began to cry, and Martha knelt down to hold her tightly to her.

The big man, on the porch steps, turned to survey the group. "I think we'd better just go down into his basement —break down the door!"

In the sudden silence the siren wailed shrilly across the night, and the ten or twelve people seemed to draw closer to one another.

Another man took a step out from the group. "Henderson's right," he said. "There isn't any time to argue or anything else. We've just got to go down there and get in!"

A chorus of voices agreed with him.

The big man walked down the steps and started around the yard toward the garage.

Harlowe shouted at him. "Wait a minute!" He raced down the steps. "God dammit—wait a minute! We all wouldn't fit in there. It'd be crazy to even try!"

Marty Weiss's voice called out plaintively, "Why don't we draw lots? Pick out *one* family."

"What difference would it make?" Harlowe said. "He won't let us in."

Henderson, the big man, looked unsure for a moment. "We could all march down there," he said, "and tell him he's got the whole street against him. We could do that."

Again, voices agreed with him.

Harlowe pushed his way through the group to stand near Henderson. "What the hell good would that do?" he asked. "I keep telling you. Even if we were to break down the door, it couldn't accommodate all of us. We'd just be killing everybody, and for no reason!"

Mrs. Henderson's voice broke in. "If it saves even one of these kids out here—I'd call that a reason."

Again, a murmur of assent came.

"Jerry," Marty Weiss said, "you know him better than any of us. You're his best friend. Why don't you go down again? Try to talk to him. Plead with him. Tell him to pick out one family—draw lots or something—"

Henderson took a long stride over to Marty. "One family— meaning yours, Weiss, huh?"

Marty whirled around toward him. "Well, why not? Why the hell not? I've got a three-month-old baby—"

"What difference does that make?" the big man's wife said. "Is your baby's life any more precious than our kids'?"

Marty Weiss turned to her. "I never said that. If you're going to start trying to argue about who deserves to live more than the next one—"

"Why don't you shut your mouth, Weiss!" Henderson

shouted at him. In wild, illogical anger he turned to the others. "That's the way it is when the foreigners come over here. Pushy, grabby, semi-Americans!"

Marty's face went white. "Why, you garbage-brained idiot, you— There's always one person—one rotten, unthinking crumb, who suddenly has to become the number-one big straw boss and decide what ancestry is acceptable that season—"

A man at the back shouted out: "It still goes, Weiss. If we've got to start hunting around for some people to disqualify—you and yours can go to the top of the list!"

"Oh, Marty!" Rebecca sobbed, feeling a surge of a different fear.

Weiss threw off her restraining arm, and started to push his way through the crowd to the man who had spoken. Jerry Harlowe had to step between them.

"Keep it up—both of you," he said, tautly. "Just keep it up—we won't need a bomb. We can slaughter each other."

"Marty!" Rebecca Weiss's voice came from the darkness near the porch. "Please. Go down to Bill's shelter again. Ask him—"

Marty turned to her. "I've already asked him. It won't do any good!"

There was the sound of the siren again—this time closer. And far off in the distance, a stabbing searchlight probed the night sky.

The Conelrad announcer's voice came up again, and they heard him repeating the same Yellow Alert announcement as before.

"Mommy, mommy!" a little girl's voice quavered. "I don't want to die, mommy! I don't want to die!"

Henderson looked at the child, then started to walk toward the garage. Gradually, in little groups, the neighbors followed him.

"I'm going down there," he announced as he walked, "and get him to open that door. I don't care what the rest of you think—that's the only thing left to do."

Another man called out: "He's right. Come on, let's do it!"

They were no longer walking. Now they were a running, jostling group, linked by positive action. And Jerry Harlowe, watching them run past him, suddenly noticed that in the moonlight all their faces looked the same—wild eyes; taut, grim, set mouths—an aura of pushing, driving ferocity.

They slammed their way through the garage, and Henderson kicked open the door leading to the basement. Like a mob of fanatics, they shouted their way into the basement.

Henderson pounded his fist on the shelter door. "Bill? Bill Stockton! You've got a bunch of your neighbors out here who want to stay alive. Now you can open that door and talk to us and figure out with us how many can come in there—or else you can just keep doing what you're doing—and we'll bust our way in!"

They all shouted in agreement.

On the other side of the door, Grace Stockton grabbed her son and held him tight. Stockton stood close to the door, for the first time unsure and frightened. Again he heard the pounding—this time by many fists.

"Come on, Stockton!" a voice called from the other side. "Open up!"

Then there was the familiar voice of Jerry Harlowe.

"Bill, this is Jerry. They mean business out here."

Stockton wet his lips. "And I mean business in here," he said. "I've already told you, Jerry—you're wasting your time. You're wasting precious time that could be used for something else . . . like figuring out how you're going to survive."

Again Henderson smashed at the door with a heavy fist, and felt the unyielding metal. He turned to look at his neighbors. "Why don't we get some kind of a battering ram?" he suggested.

"That's right," another man said. "We could go over to Bennett Avenue. Phil Kline has a bunch of two-by-fours in his basement. I've seen them."

A woman's protesting voice, somehow petulant and ugly, broke in. "That would get him into the act," her voice said. "And who cares about saving *him*! The minute we do that, then we'll let all those people know that there's a shelter on this street. We'd have a whole mob to contend with. A whole bunch of outsiders."

"Sure," Mrs. Henderson agreed. "And what right do they have to come over here? This isn't *their* street. This isn't *their* shelter."

Jerry Harlowe stared from one silhouette to another and wondered what insane logic possessed them all.

"This is our shelter, huh?" he cried fiercely. "And on the next street—that's a different country. Patronize home industries! You idiots! You goddam fools! You're insane now —all of you."

"Maybe you don't want to live," Rebecca Weiss's voice cried out. "Maybe you don't care, Jerry."

"I care," Harlowe said to her. "Believe me, I care. I'd like to see the morning come, too. But you've become a mob. And a mob doesn't have any brains, and that's what you're proving. That's what you're proving right at this moment— that you don't have any brains."

Henderson's voice spoke—harsh, loud. "I say let's get a battering ram!" he shouted, like a cheer leader. "And we'll just tell Kline to keep his mouth shut as to why we want it."

"I agree with Jerry." Marty Weiss's voice was tentative and diffident. "Let's get hold of ourselves. Let's stop and think for a minute—"

Henderson turned to face Weiss's small dark form. "Nobody cares what you think!" He spit it out. "You or your kind. I thought I made it clear upstairs. I think the first order of business is to get you out of here."

He moved in on Marty and lashed out with the force of two hundred pounds. His fist smashed against Marty Weiss's cheek and Marty fell backward, landing first against a woman, then stumbling against a child, and finally winding up on his back. His wife screamed and started running toward him —and the whole dark basement echoed and re-echoed with the sound of angry shouts and frightened cries, sparked by the wail of a terror-stricken child.

"Come on!" Henderson's bull voice carried over the noise. "Let's go get something to smash this door down."

They were a mob, and they moved like a mob. Fear had become fury. Panic had become resolve. They stormed out of the basement onto the street. Each was willing to follow his neighbor. Each was content to let someone else lead. And while they marched wildly down the street, the voice of the Conelrad announcer darted like a thin menacing needle in and out of their consciousness.

"We have been asked to remind the population once again," the announcer's voice said, "that they are to remain calm. Stay off the streets. This is urgent. Please remain off the streets. Everything possible is being done in the way of protection, but the military cannot move, and important Civil Defense vehicles must have the streets clear. So you're once again reminded to stay off the streets. *Remain off the streets.*"

But the crowd continued down the block. They were not listening to the words that the radio said. There was an emergency, and the radio made it official.

Less than five minutes later, they were back in front of Stockton's house. They had found a long board and six men were carrying it. They took it into the garage, breaking a window in the door as they entered. Then they used it to smash the door into the basement. They carried it through the basement over to the shelter door and began to pound against it. The shelter door was thick—but not thick enough. The weight of the board, with six big men at it, first dented and then punctured the metal. And once the first rip appeared, others followed it, until, within moments, the top hinge had been smashed away and the door began to buckle.

Inside, Bill Stockton tried to pile cots, a chair, other furniture, and finally the generator, against it. But with each smashing, resounding blow, the barricade was pushed back.

The door finally gave and crashed into the shelter. The impetus of the final blow carried board and men into the room, and the side of the board grazed Stockton's head, tearing out a chunk of flesh.

Suddenly everyone was silent, and over this sudden silence came the sound of the siren—a long, piercing blast which gradually died away—and then the voice of the radio announcer came on again.

"This is Conelrad," the announcer's voice said. "This is Conelrad. Remain tuned for an important message. Remain tuned for an important message."

There was a silence for a moment, and then the voice continued. "The President of the United States has just announced that the previously unidentified objects have now been definitely identified as being satellites. Repeat. There are no enemy missiles approaching. Repeat. There are no enemy missiles approaching. The objects have been identified as satellites. They are harmless, and we are in no danger. Repeat. We are in no danger. The state of Yellow Alert has been cancelled. The state of Yellow Alert has been cancelled. We are in no danger. Repeat. There is no enemy attack. There is no enemy attack."

His voice continued, the words at first having no sense to the listeners, then gradually taking on form and meaning.

And then men turned to look at their wives and slowly took them in their arms. Small children buried their faces against trousered and skirted legs. There were some sobs, some murmured prayers. The lights came on again in the streets and houses and the men and women stared at one another.

"Thank God." Rebecca Weiss's voice was a prayer for them all. "Oh, thank God."

She leaned against Marty, only vaguely aware that his lip was torn and bleeding.

"Amen," said Marty. "Amen."

Henderson kept staring at his big hands as if they were something he had never seen. Then he swallowed and turned to Weiss.

"Hey, Marty," he said, softly, with a thin smile. "Marty . . . I went off my rocker. You understand that, don't you? I just went off my rocker. I didn't mean all the things I said." His voice shook. "We were all of us . . . we were so scared. We were so confused."

He waved his hands helplessly. "Well, it's no wonder really, is it? I mean . . . well . . . you can understand why we blew our tops a little."

There was a murmur of voices, a few perfunctory nods, but the state of shock was still on them.

Jerry Harlowe left the basement steps and walked to the center of the cellar. "I don't think Marty's gonna hold it against you." He turned toward Stockton, who stood motionless at the entrance to the shelter. "Just as I hope Bill won't hold *this* against us," Harlowe continued, pointing to the wreckage and rubble around him. "We'll pay for the damage, Bill. We'll take up a collection right away."

Marty Weiss wiped the blood off his mouth. "Why don't we have some kind of a block party or something tomorrow night?" he said. "A big celebration! How about that? Just like old times."

The people stared at him.

"So we can all of us get back to normal," he continued. "How about it, Bill?"

Every eye turned to Stockton, who stood there silently looking at them.

Harlowe dredged up a laugh. "Hey, Bill . . . I told you we'd pay for the damages. I'll put that in writing if you want."

The silence persisted as Stockton stepped over the broken door and walked into the basement area. He looked around him as if trying to find someone in particular. He felt the throbbing at the side of his head as he walked past the faces of neighbors. Their eyes followed him as he went on over to the cellar steps.

"Bill," Harlowe whispered. "Hey, Bill—"

Stockton turned to him. "That's all it takes," he said. "That's all it takes, huh?" he said. He looked at Marty Weiss. "Marty," he said, "you want a block party and you want things back to normal. And Frank Henderson, over there—he wants us all to forget all about it. Chalk it up to a bad scare. And, Jerry—you'll pay for the damages, huh? You'll even put it in writing. You'll pay for the damages . . ."

Harlowe nodded silently.

Stockton looked slowly around the room. "Do any of you have any remote idea just what the 'damages' are?" He paused. "Let me tell you something. They're more than that broken door there. And they're a lot deeper than the bruises on Marty Weiss's face. And you don't wipe them out by throwing a block party—or a hundred block parties, every night of the year."

He saw his wife step out of the shelter, and then his son Paul. They were staring at him with the others. The same questioning look. The same beaten and somehow haunted look. Stockton put his hand on the railing.

"The damages I'm talking about," he said, "are the pieces of ourselves that we've pulled apart tonight. The veneer—the thin veneer that we ripped aside with our own hands. The hatred that came to the surface that we didn't even realize we had. But, oh Jesus—how quick it came out! And how quickly we became animals! All of us."

He pointed to himself. "Me, too—maybe I was the worst of the bunch. I don't know."

He paused for a moment and looked around. "I don't think it'll be normal again. At least, not in our lifetime. And if, God forgive, that bomb does fall—I hope we've made our peace *before* we suffer it. I hope that if it has to kill and destroy and maim, the victims will be human beings—not naked, wild beasts who put such a premium on staying alive that they claw their neighbors to death just for the privilege."

He shook his head and then, very slowly, turned to look up toward the kitchen. "That's what the damage has been," he said, and he started up the steps. "It's having to look at ourselves in a mirror and see what's underneath the skin, and suddenly realizing that underneath . . . we're an ugly race of people."

He went up the steps, and after a moment, Grace, holding

tight to Paul's hand, moved through the silent people and followed him.

The silence stretched to a long moment, and then gradually, by two's and three's, the neighbors started out of the basement, through the garage and onto the street.

The street lights were bright, and the moon was up and high and full. A radio that had been left on blared out dance-band music. A television set once again uttered the canned laughter of a manufactured audience. A child cried, but was crooned to and hushed. It was any summer night again. There was the sound of the cicadas. There was the croaking rumble of distant bullfrogs. There was a gentle wind that touched the broad leaves with a rustling sound and sent patches of shadow criss-crossing on the sidewalks.

Bill Stockton stood in the dining room. At his feet was the remnant of the birthday cake lying on its side. A few broken candles, snuffed out, lay in a crumble of frosting. And he thought that for humanity to survive . . . the human race must remain civilized.

Funny, he thought, as he walked past the smashed, over-turned furniture—really quite funny, how a simple thing like that could have eluded him.

He took his wife's hand, and then Paul's, and the three of them started up the stairs to their beds.

The night had ended.

SHOWDOWN
WITH
RANCE
McGREW

THE two cowboys walked out of the saloon down the three steps of the front porch and stood there peering down the length of the dusty main street. One of them spat out a blob of brown liquid, then wiped his beard-stubbled chin.

"He ain't here yet," he announced.

His companion took out a pocket watch and snapped it open.

"He will be. He knows what's waitin' for him!"

He snapped the watch shut and put it back into his leather vest.

The first cowboy squinted into the sun. "He's gonna get shot this mornin'," he announced laconically. "There ain't no doubt about that."

The second cowboy grunted in assent, then watched his friend stick another chunk of brown stuff into his mouth. "What is that?" he inquired.

"Hershey bar," his companion said, "but the damn thing is stale and it don't have no nuts in it neither."

There came the sound of a roar. It was at first distant, like a far-off growl, then it built up until it was a full-throated shriek—and around the corner came a red Jaguar, chrome-spoked wheels churning their way through the dust, and screaming their protest as the car turned more sharply and headed down the main street. It threw up tons of dust as once again the driver jerked it abruptly to the right and slammed on the brakes. The car plowed to a stop a foot from the porch of the saloon, squatting there like some low-slung red animal. A horse tethered next to it stared at the driver, snorted, and looked away.

Rance McGrew climbed carefully out of the front seat, swiped the dust off his cream-colored whipcord pants and white silk shirt, straightened the black and yellow ascot around his neck, and carefully tilted the brim of his white Stetson. He kicked the car door shut and started up the steps of the saloon.

"Howdy, Mr. McGrew," one of the cowboys said.

"Howdy," Rance answered, clutching at the post at the top of the steps as one of his boots turned inward, and he teetered momentarily.

Rance wore the only elevator boots in the business, with two-inch lifts inside and three-inch heels on the bottom. This shot him up to five feet seven.

The door to the saloon opened and Sy Blattsburg came out. He was a bald, dapper little man in a sport shirt. The shirt was soaked with perspiration. He looked worriedly at his wrist watch and then at Rance.

"You're an hour and fifteen minutes late, Rance," he announced with suppressed anger. "We should've had this scene all shot by now."

Rance shrugged his shoulders under their padding, and swaggered past him through the swinging doors into the make-believe saloon, where a camera crew and a party of extras sat around looking relieved and bored at the same time.

Sy Blattsburg, who had spent twenty years directing all kinds of phony-balonies, followed this particular phony-baloney into the saloon. "Makeup," he called, as he padded after the star.

The makeup man hurried onto the scene. Forcing a beatific smile at the "cowboy," he pointed to the wooden stool in front of the makeup mirror.

"Right over here, Mr. McGrew," he said pleasantly.

Rance sat down on the stool and surveyed his reflection.

"Make it kind of quick, will you?" the director said, his lips twitching ever so slightly. "We're quite a bit behind, Rance—"

Rance turned, knocking the powder puff out of the makeup man's hand. "Don't bug me, Sy," he said with a fast burn. "You know what emotional scenes do to me just before we shoot!"

The director smiled and closed his eyes, then patted the star on his padded shoulders. "Don't get upset, Rance baby. We'll try to knock this one out in a hurry. What do you say we get started—huh? Okay, baby? This is scene seventy-one."

He snapped his fingers and the script girl handed him the manuscript. "Here it is, right here," he said, pointing to one of the pages.

Rance languidly held out his hand and Blattsburg gave him the script. Rance looked at it briefly, then gave it back. "Read it to me," he said.

Blattsburg cleared his throat. His hand shook as he clutched at the script. "Interior saloon," he read. "Cover shot of two badmen at bar. Rance McGrew enters. He walks to bar. He glances sideways left and right."

Rance pushed the makeup man's arm away and turned slowly to stare at the director. " 'He glances sideways left and right?' Is my head supposed to be built on a swivel?"

He grabbed the script out of the director's hand. "I'm gonna tell you something, Sy," he announced. "When a cowboy walks into a bar, he walks to the far end of the room. He takes his drink. He looks at it. Then he looks straight ahead. He doesn't look left and right."

With this, Rance McGrew turned back toward the mirror, his face white under the powdered makeup, his lips twitching. His large baby-blue eyes clouded like those of a high-school sophomore cheer leader whose megaphone had just been dented.

Sy Blattsburg closed his eyes again. He knew only too well the tone of Rance McGrew's voice and he was also familiar with the look on the face. It boded no good—either for that moment or for the day's schedule.

"All right, Rance," he said softly. "We'll shoot it your way. Any way you want." He wet his lips. "Now can we begin?"

"In a moment," Rance said, his eyes half closed in what appeared to be a very special and personal agony. "In just a moment. My stomach's killing me. These scenes," he said, as one hand massaged his belly. "These miserable emotional scenes."

He pointed to a large hide-covered box on the floor near him. There, in hand-stitched elegance, was the name "Rance McGrew." Two stars were underneath it. A prop boy opened it up and rummaged through its interior. There were bottles of medicine, throat lozenges, sprays, and a large stack of autographed publicity pictures of Rance fanning a six-gun. The prop boy took out one of the bottles of pills and brought it over to the makeup chair.

Rance opened the bottle and popped two of the pills into his mouth, swallowing them whole. Then he sat quietly for a moment—the makeup man waiting motionless. Rance slowly opened his eyes and nodded, whereupon the makeup man continued his ministrations.

Fifty-odd people began quietly setting up the scene. The

cameraman checked the position of his camera, nodded his approval to the operator, and everyone turned to look expectantly toward Sy Blattsburg.

Sy checked the angle of the camera, and then called, "Second team out! The star is here!"

Rance McGrew's stand-in left his place close to the swinging doors and Sy turned toward Rance.

"All set, Rance baby," he said diffidently. "And we'll shoot it just the way you want."

Rance McGrew rose slowly from his wooden stool and stood looking at himself in the mirror. The makeup man put on the final touches of powder. A wardrobe man puttered around his leather vest.

Rance, still looking at himself, cocked his head, snapped his fingers, and pointed to one shoulder. The wardrobe man hurriedly inserted an inch of additional padding. Again Rance stared into the mirror and then snapped his fingers again. "Holster," he said tersely.

A property man trotted to his side and began to tie on his holster.

Rance checked it by holding one arm straight down at his side and sighting down at it. "An inch more hang," he ordered.

The property man quickly obeyed, loosening the belt one notch as Rance checked himself again in the mirror, moving his head around so that he could survey himself from several different angels. He stepped away from the mirror and then advanced on it, arms held away from his body in the manner of every fast gun since the beginning of time.

It might be parenthetically noted here that there was a point in history when there actually were top guns. They were a motley collection of tough mustaches who galloped and gunned their way across the then new West. They left behind them a raft of legends and legerdemains. But heroics or hambone—it can be stated quite definitely that they were a rough and woolly breed of nail-eaters who in matters of the gun were as efficient as they were dedicated. It does seem a reasonable guess, however, that if there were any television sets up in Cowboy Heaven, so that these worthies could see with what careless abandon their names and exploits were being bandied about—not to mention the fact that each week they were killed off afresh by Jaguar-drawn Hollywood tigers who couldn't distinguish between a holster and hoof and mouth disease—they were very likely turning over in their graves or, more drastically, getting out of them.

None of this, of course, occurred to Rance McGrew as he swaggered across the set to the bat-wing doors, losing his balance only once or twice as his boots gave slightly to the left—much in the manner of a nine-year-old Brownie wearing her mother's high heels.

When Rance reached the swinging doors he squared his padded shoulders, snapped his fingers again, and ordered tersely: *"My gun."* This, of course, was the final item in the ritual of Rance McGrew's preparation, and it occurred at the same time each morning. The prop man pitched underhanded an ugly-looking six-shooter which Rance caught deftly, spun around on the trigger finger of his right hand, and then with equal deftness flipped it to his left hand. He then let it spin over his shoulder, putting his right hand behind him to catch it. The ugly-looking six-shooter didn't know about the plan. It sailed swiftly over Rance, over the cameraman, over the bartender, and slammed against the bar mirror, smashing it into a million pieces.

Sy Blattsburg shut his eyes tightly and wiped the sweat from his face. With a heroic effort, he kept his voice low and untroubled. "Dress it up," he ordered. "We'll wait for the new glass." He pulled out a five-dollar bill and handed it to the cameraman.

He had now lost four hundred and thirty-five dollars over the three-year span of Rance McGrew's television show. In one hundred and eighteen films, this was the eighty-fourth time that Rance has broken the bar mirror.

Twenty minutes later the set had been dressed and a new mirror put up. Blattsburg stood alongside the cameraman. "All right," he said, "ready . . . action!"

The camera began its quiet hum. Outside a horse whinnied, and through the swinging doors swaggered Rance McGrew in simple, powdered elegance, a noncommittal sneer on his face. The two "bad guys" stood at the bar and watched fearfully as he approached them. Rance went up to the bar and slammed the palm of his hand down on top of it.

"Rotgut whiskey," he said in a deep voice, perhaps one octave lower than Johnny Weissmuller's. And while he may have walked like a Brownie, Rance's ordinary speaking voice was that of a grocery boy in the middle of a voice change.

The bartender yanked a bottle from the shelf and slid it down the length of the bar. Rance nonchalantly held out his hand for it and looked mildly surprised as the bottle sped past him to break against the wall where the bar ended.

Sy Blattsburg jammed both his thumbs into his eyes and stood shaking for a moment. "Cut," he said finally.

There was a murmur of reaction from the crew. It was traditional that Rance missed at least one bottle that was slid toward him, but this usually occurred toward the end of the day when he was tired.

The sneer on his face turned a shade petulant as he waggled a finger toward the bartender. "All right, buddy boy," he said warningly. "You try to gag it up one more time and you'll wind up plucking chickens at a market!"

He turned toward the director. "He put an English on that, Sy. He deliberately made it curve."

The bartender gaped at the two "bad guys."

"English on a bottle?" he whispered incredulously. "That guy needs a catcher's mitt!"

With masterful control, Blattsburg said quietly, "All right. Let's try it again. From the bottle. Positions, please."

"Scene seventy-three—take two," a voice called out.

Again the bartender pulled down a bottle and very carefully nudged it so that it slid along the bar slowly and stopped dead, a hand's length away.

Rance's lips curled in one of his best sneers. He reached for the bottle, picked it up, slammed it against the edge of the bar, and then raised the jagged neck to his mouth, drinking thirstily. He threw the bottle over his shoulder, probed at one of his back teeth with his tongue, and finally, rather showily, removed a large fragment of fake glass from his mouth. This he flipped toward the bartender and his mail-order sneer returned to his face.

He leaned against the bar, wiggling his shoulders, and surveyed the two "bad guys." At the same time, he carefully checked his reflection in the mirror and tilted his Stetson an inch or so to the right.

"I guess you boys know I'm the marshal here," he announced in his best Boot Hill voice.

The two "bad guys" were visibly shaken.

"We heard tell," the first one said, not daring to meet Marshal McGrew's gaze.

"We heard tell," the other cowboy chimed in.

Rance lifted one eyebrow and stared from one to the other. "And I guess you know that I know that Jesse James is due here, aimin' to call on me."

The first cowboy nodded and his voice shook.

"I knew that, too," he said fearfully.

"Likewise," his companion added.

Rance stood there for a quiet moment, moving his head left and right, the sneer coming and going.

"Somethin' else I know that you two don't know," he said, "is that I know that both of you know Jesse James. And I'm waitin'—I'm jus' gonna stand here waitin'."

The two "desperadoes" exchanged horrified stares, and with all the subtlety of a grade C wrestler they looked worriedly toward the swinging doors. This was Rance's cue to move away from the bar, hands held down and ready at his sides.

The sneer now came with a smile. "I figgered I'd bluff ya," he said triumphantly. "Jesse's here all right, ain't he?"

"Marshal . . ." the bartender pleaded. "Marshal McGrew . . . please . . . no killin' in here!"

Rance held up his hand for quiet. "I ain't aimin' to kill 'im," he announced gently. "I'm jus' gonna maim 'im a bit. I'm jus' gonna pick off his pinky!"

The first "desperado" swallowed and gulped. "J-J-Jesse ain't gonna take kindly to that," he stuttered.

Out on the street there was the sound of hoofs, the creak of leather, and then boot-steps across the wooden floor of the saloon porch.

The swinging doors opened, and there stood Jesse James —evil incarnate. Black mustache, black pants and shirt, black gloves, black scarf, and black hat. His particular sneer was closely related to Rance's, though not worn with the aplomb of the marshal.

He walked across the saloon with catlike grace, hands held down and away from his body.

"It's Marshal McGrew, ain't it?" he asked, planting his legs far apart, his hands still out—elbows bent.

Rance McGrew sneered, sniggered, clucked, and breathed heavily, and finally said, "Yup."

"You're about to breathe your last, marshal."

Then Jesse went for his gun. Halfway out of the holster a simulated bullet drew simulated blood from his hand, which he clutched in agony as his gun flew off to one side.

The prop man blew smoke out of the chamber of the blank-cartridge pistol.

Sy Blattsburg nodded approvingly.

The two cowboys at the bar reacted with proper horror.

The extras sitting at the tables jumped to their feet and moved slowly backwards toward the wall.

Meanwhile, back at the bar, Rance McGrew was still tugging at the gun in his holster. It finally came out, left his

hand, and kept going over his shoulder, over the cameraman, over the bartender, smack dab into the mirror, breaking
it into a million pieces.

Sy Blattsburg looked as if someone had told him that he
had just become engaged to a lizard, he opened his mouth
and a noise akin to a sob—a protest, a throttled roar—
came out. When he got control of himself, he said quite
clearly, "Cut!"

He turned toward the cameraman and giggled. Then he
just sat down and began to cry.

And so it went through the day. They shot Rance grappling
with Jesse until Jesse hauled back to let the marshal have it
on his sneer. Rance's stand-in took his place to receive the
blow, and then fell backward to land on top of a collapsing
table.

There was some exceptional footage of Rance throwing
Jesse over the bar to smash against a shelf full of bottles;
then the action called for Jesse to climb up on top of the bar
and dive over it into the on-coming Rance. Rance's stand-in
again took the brunt of this assault, stepping in in time to
receive the full weight of Jesse James hurtling through the
air at him.

By late afternoon Rance began to show the effect of four
hours of mortal combat. Sweat showed through his powder.
His stand-in had half his shirt ripped off, a large mouse under
his left eye, and three dislocated knuckles.

Rance patted him on the shoulder as he passed by. "Good
show," he said bravely, like a Bengal Lancer talking to a
doomed drummer boy.

"Yes sir, Mr. McGrew," his stand-in said through bruised
lips.

Sy Blattsburg checked his watch, then walked to the center
of the room. "All right, boys," he announced. "This is the
death scene—Rance stands at the bar, Jesse lies over there.
Rance thinks he's unconscious. Jesse picks a gun off the
floor and fires at Rance's back."

The actor playing Jesse James looked up startled. "At his
back?" he said.

"That's right," Blattsburg responded.

"I don't want to fight you, Sy," the actor said, "but that's
not the way Jesse James used to operate. I mean . . . everything I've read about the guy, he fought pretty fair. Why
can't I yell something?"

Rance McGrew's upper lip curled. "That's thinking," he
said with devastating sarcasm. "Oh, that's thinking. Yell

something. Warn the fastest gun in the West that he's about to be shot at."

Rance took a step over and poked a finger against the actor's chest. "You happen to be up against Rance McGrew," he snarled. "And when you're up against Rance McGrew you've got to play it dirty or you're gonna play it dead. Now quit arguing and let's get to it!"

The actor looked over at Sy Blattsburg, who made a gesture of a finger to his mouth.

As the actor walked past him, Sy said, "Jesse James might not fight that way—but," he continued in a whisper, "Rance McGrew would!"

Once again the extras took their places at the tables. Jesse James lay down in a chalked-off spot on the floor and Rance McGrew stood by the bar, his back to his adversary. The property man put a bottle in front of him and Rance sniffed at it. Once again his upper lip curled.

"I told you ginger ale!" he screeched. "This goddamn stuff is coke!"

The property man looked worriedly at the director. "It's supposed to look like whisky though, Mr. McGrew, and—"

Rance's shriek cut him off. "Sy! Will you fire this oaf—or straighten him out—one or the other?"

Sy Blattsburg stepped in front of the camera. His voice was gentle. "Mr. McGrew would prefer ginger ale."

The property man heaved a deep sigh. "Yes sir, Mr. McGrew."

Jesse James, lying on the floor, whispered to the director: "I don't care what he says—Jesse James wouldn't shoot anybody in the back."

Sy gritted his teeth. "Yeah, I know, but Rance McGrew would. Rance McGrew would also fire anybody and his brother. So do me a favor—play it Rance McGrew's way or we'll never get this picture finished."

"All right. You're the boss, but I can just see Jesse James turning over in his grave now. I don't mean just once. I mean about four hundred revolutions per minute."

Sy Blattsburg nodded and shrugged. "All right," he called out. "Let's get with it. Scene ninety-three, take one."

The camera began to hum and Blattsburg called out "Action!"

Rance McGrew reached for the bottle, smashed it open, held it out, and looked in the mirror. He could see the reflection of the crew, the cameramen, the director, and, naturally, Rance McGrew. He put the shattered bottle to his mouth and took a long, deep swig. Then the bottle fell from his hands. His eyes bulged. He choked, gasped, and clutched at his throat.

"Why, you stupid bastard—that's whisky! *That's real whisky!*"

Again he looked up toward the mirror, and this time what made him gasp was not the burning liquid pouring down his throat. It was what he saw in the mirror. Just himself. Himself and two strangers—two dirty-looking cowboys standing a few feet away from him.

One of the hostesses sat with customers at the table, but it wasn't the long-legged blonde who was there before. It was a fat, dumpy, frowsy-looking babe on the corseted side of fifty-five.

Rance kept opening and shutting his eyes, then started to say something to the bartender when he realized that this gentleman, too, had changed. He was no longer the fat, waddling, bald-headed man cast in the role. He was a thin, chicken-chested little guy with his hair parted in the middle. He stared back at Rance questioningly.

Rance stumbled back from the bar and stared upward. There had been no real ceiling—just a series of catwalks where some of the lighting men had been positioned. Now there was no catwalk—just a plain old ceiling.

Marshal McGrew continued to walk backward until he felt the swinging doors behind him. He kept on going and wound up on the street just as an old man ran breathlessly toward him. An old man he'd never seen before.

"Marshal," the grizzled octogenarian wheezed at him, "Jesse's gunnin' for you. He's comin' right now!"

"Cement head!" Rance shrieked back at him. "He already came in—scene seventy-three. Goddamn it—will my agent hear about this! Will the head of the studio hear about this!" He pounded on his small chest. "Try to get *me* for another benefit! Boy, am I gonna tell you something!"

He pointed toward the old man and then stopped breathing before his words came out, for down the street a horse ambled slowly toward him. And on the horse was a tall lean man in a black costume—his hawk face shadowed by the black broad-brimmed hat.

Any real student of the West would at this moment have died of a coronary, because the face was that of Jesse James. Not the actor—but Jesse James.

The horse stopped a few feet from where Rance stood and the rider dismounted, looked up and down the street, and then slowly came over toward the marshal.

The marshal, meanwhile, found himself sitting on the steps of the saloon unable to move.

The tall dark man stood over him and surveyed him intently.

"They call me Jesse James," the deep voice said. "I mean the *real* Jesse James—not that side of pork that's been play-actin' me!"

Silence—except for the plop-plop sound of Rance McGrew's sweat that kept running down the bridge of his nose and landing in the dust. Finally Rance looked up, his eyes glazed.

"Cut?" he inquired. "Shouldn't we cut?" His voice was tearful. "Please somebody—cut already!"

But nothing happened. The apparition under the black hat remained. No makeup man came to dab off the marshal's perspiration. No stunt man stood on the periphery ready to save him from the least damage. Marshal McGrew was all alone.

"I'm lookin' fer the marshal in town," Jesse James said. "Fella named McGrew. Rance McGrew."

Rance very slowly tipped his hat down over his face and stuck out his left hand, pointing down the street. "That-away," he announced.

"You wouldn't be him, huh?" Jesse asked.

Rance shook his head and continued to point down the street, but suddenly Jesse lashed out with both hands, grabbed Rance by the front of his vest, and yanked him to his feet. Holding him with one hand, he tapped the shiny badge adorning Rance's costume and looked accusingly into the pale, perspiring face of the law man.

Rance gulped, swallowed, and started to take off the vest —looking wildly around. "Where's the fellow who lent me this?" he inquired weakly.

Jesse stopped him in the middle of his activities and pulled him closer.

"I think you and me better have a talk, marshal. Mebbe a long talk, mebbe a short talk—but a talk."

He slowly released Rance and continued to stare at him.

"You're supposed to be tough," he said thoughtfully. "Ya don't look very tough. Wanna know what ya look like?"

"I haven't been well," Rance answered in a thin little voice.

Jesse nodded. "You look like a marshmallow." Then he

paused and stepped back. "Don't that rile ya none?" he asked.

Marshal McGrew smiled at him with a wispy "when-are-they-gonna-let-me-commit-suicide?" kind of smile.

Jesse shrugged. "C'mon," he ordered. "First we'll have a drink, and then we'll have a talk." There was a meaningful pause. "Then we'll have a showdown."

He herded Rance up the steps and into the saloon. Once inside, he shoved him up against the bar.

"Two whiskies," Jesse said, "and leave the bottles."

The bartender slid one bottle down the bar and Jesse backhanded it like Roy McMillan. The other bottle Rance laboriously stopped with both hands. Habit made him instinctively smash it against the bar—not once but five times, with no tangible results. This bottle was made of sterner stuff than the marshal was accustomed to. On the sixth smash, however, he finally managed to crack it, and on the seventh he wound up holding a small piece of glass and a cork. The rest of the bottle, and its contents, were in a puddle at his feet.

Rance looked up guiltily toward Jesse James, who stared at him like a scientist checking a bug under a microscope.

"Marshmallow!" Jesse spat in disgust.

He tilted his own bottle to his lips and took a long draught. He threw the bottle over his shoulder and reached inside his vest for a sack of tobacco and a pack of cigarette papers. He opened the sack and expertly poured an exact amount on the paper, rolled it between thumb and two fingers into a neat cylinder, licked the edge, rolled it again, caught the string of the tobacco sack in his teeth and pulled it closed, twisted one end of the cigarette shut, pasted the other to his lower lip, scratched a big wooden match with his thumbnail, and lit up. He then threw the makings—sack, paper, and another match—over to Rance McGrew, who immediately started to open the sack with his teeth, got the string caught between two of his molars, sneezed, and after much laborious finagling managed to spill a small thumbnail-ful of tobacco onto the paper. He then kneaded, pressed, tamped, and licked, put the cigarette to his mouth, and discovered that the tobacco had run out of the open end.

Rance shamefacedly pried the string out of his teeth, then stopped to think about what to do with the empty piece of paper stuck to the side of his mouth.

Jesse decided it for him. He backhanded the paper into the air, then looked a little dolefully at McGrew, shook his head, and said, "You don't do nothin' well, do ya, McGrew?"

He took a deep luxurious drag on his cigarette and blew

the smoke into Rance's left eye. After waiting a moment for some reaction—and there was none except a small tear—he shook his head again.

"Don't that rile ya?" he asked.

Rance smiled at him and coughed out a piece of tobacco.

"Nothin' riles ya, does it?" Jesse James said. "You're the most even-tempered dude I ever did meet. However," he continued, blowing smoke out again, "I ain't got no more time to be social, marshal. I believe it's time to come to a meetin' of the minds."

He took a step away from the bar and immediately the people at the table made a collective dash to neutral corners.

It was, Rance thought to himself, like every movie he'd ever seen—and he reflected further that this couldn't be happening. Eventually he'd wake up. But he couldn't wake up, because the thing went right on happening.

Jesse James nodded toward the frightened onlookers. "Why d'ya suppose they're gettin' under cover, marshal?"

Rance gulped. "I think the place is closing." He looked around a little wildly. "Yep—it's curfew time!"

Again he gulped, winked, smiled, and then with a kind of skipping gait headed toward the door. "Mighty nice mettin' ya, Mr. James . . . Jesse."

He was at the swinging doors when Jesse's voice stopped him.

"Marshal," Jesse said, "jus' stop right there!"

The voice was like a lasso that circled around Rance's legs and held him tightly. He slowly turned to face Jesse, who had reached out with his foot and pulled a chair over.

"You wasn't leavin', was ya, marshal?" Jesse asked as he sat down. "I mean . . . you wasn't jus' gonna up and walk out, was ya?"

Rance smiled at him like some village idiot. "Nope," he answered, "I was just wonderin' if it was gonna rain."

He turned to stare out very professionally toward the street, then turned back to Billy. "Nope," he said firmly, "it ain't gonna rain."

Jesse laughed, and then tipped his chair back. "D'ya know what I thought, marshal?" he said. "I thought you was gonna play some kinda trick on me. Remember the time that bad guy had ya covered in the back and ya started out the swingin' doors and ya swung one door back and knocked the gun outta his hand?"

"That was the opening show last season," Rance interjected.

"Or how about when that rustlin' gang had collected in here to bushwhack ya—ten or eleven of 'em?"

Rance smiled in fond recollection. "Thirteen," he said. "I was up for an Emmy on that one."

Jesse nodded, and when he spoke he sounded grim. "That was when ya shot from the hip and brung down the chandelier." He shook his head. "That was some shootin', marshal."

Rance was wistful. "I did better the next week. Horse thief named McNasty. Shot a glass outta his hand, bullet ricocheted and hit his confederate out there on the porch. I got thirteen hundred pieces of mail on that one."

Jesse nodded again. "I bet you did. I bet you did, indeed. Why, folks jus' couldn't help admirin' a man of your talents."

Then he laughed again—first a low chuckle, and then a tremendous booming explosion.

Again Rance smiled back at him—with the kind of smile that on a baby indicates gas.

"Thing of it is, marshal," Jesse James continued, "thing of it is, I don't reckon you ever fired a real gun in your life, did ya? Or hit a man in anger? Or mebbe even got hit in anger, yourself?" He leaned forward in the chair. "Tell me true, marshal. Ever ride a horse?"

Rance cleared his throat. "On occasion."

"A real horse?"

"Well—" Rance fidgeted, scratching himself. "I happen to be allergic—hives."

"Hives?"

Rance went through a series of extravagant gestures, indicating the torture of urticaria. "You know—itching. Cats give it to me, too."

Jesse leaned back in his chair. "So ya don't ride," he said, "ya don't shoot, ya don't fight. Ya jus' strut around wearin' a phony badge and goin' through the motions of killin' off fellas like me."

"Oh, I wouldn't say that," Rance said. "There was one episode when we let one of the James boys get off. It was kind of . . . kind of a complicated plot."

He walked over toward Jesse James and pulled a chair up close to him. "It seems that there was a kid sister going to school in the East. She came out to visit him on the day he was supposed to be hanged. She appealed to me and I saw to it that he got a suspended sentence."

Jesse stared at Rance, unsmiling. "I know about it," Jesse said. "I also know how you captured 'im. Jumped eight hundred feet off a cliff to land on the back of his hoss when he wasn't lookin'." He shook his head from side to side. "Now, c'mon, marshal. You ever jump eight hundred feet off a cliff to land on a man's hoss?"

Rance looked pale. "Heights . . . heights bother me," he said weakly.

Jesse nodded. "That figgers. So ya see, marshal—we had this meetin', up there and all of us decided—my brother Frank and me, Billy the Kid, the Dalton boys, Sam Starr . . . quite a few of us—and the consensus was, marshal . . . was that you wasn't doin' a thing for our good names. We had a little election up there and they chose me to come down and mebbe take a little shine offa your pants!"

Rance stared at him. "How's that?" he asked.

"Don'cha get it? We see ya week after week shootin' down this fella, shootin' down that fella—capturin' that bushwhacker, capturin' that rustler—but alla time winnin'! Man, you jus' don't never lose. You're the winnin'est fella ever come down the pike, and that's for sure. So, me 'n' my friends —well, we figgered how it was about time that mebbe you lost one time!"

Rance swallowed hard. "That's not such a bad idea. I could take it up with the producer." His voice was hopeful.

Jesse shook his head. "I don't think there's time fer that," he said firmly. "I think that mebbe if you're gonna lose, you're gonna have to lose right now!" He rose from the chair slowly and then kicked it away. "But I'll tell ya what I'm gonna do, marshal. I'm gonna play it square with ya. A whole helluva lot squarer than you ever played it with us. Face to face and no—how you call em?—stunt men."

He pointed out toward the street. "Right out there on the main street—you 'n' me."

Rance pointed to himself with a limp hand. "Me?" he asked.

"Right outside," Jesse continued. "Me comin' down one side of the street—you comin' down the other."

Rance gestured a little forlornly. "It's been done before. You didn't happen to see 'Gunfight at O.K. Corral,' did you?"

Jesse James spat on the floor. "Lousy!" he said, like a judge pronouncing sentence.

"Didn't care for it, huh?" Rance cleared his throat, tapped his fingertips together. "It's always been my belief," he said, "that when shooting a western—"

Jesse James lifted him up off his chair and placed him hard on his feet. "Let's go, marshal," he said.

He gave him a shove and Rance stumbled out through the swinging doors, followed by Jesse and by the crowd in the saloon. Jesse shoved him again and he tumbled down the steps.

Again Rance thought: This must be the tail end of a bad dream. He'd wake up sleeping in his Jaguar. There—right there in front of those steps was where he had parked it. Only it wasn't there now, of course.

Jesse gave him a push and pointed toward one end of the street. "You come around that corner," he directed Rance, "and I'll come around that one." He jerked his thumb over his shoulder. "I'll let ya make the first move. Now, nothin' could be fairer than that, marshal, could it?"

"Oh, my, no," Rance answered. "No, indeed. Nothing at all." Then he very busily looked at his wrist watch. "How about tomorrow afternoon—same time?"

This time Jesse pushed him with more verve and Rance fell over his own elevator boots, banging his knees as he landed.

"*This afternoon!*" Jesse said to the U. S. Marshal in the dust. "*Right now!*"

Rance was reasonably sure that he could never rise to his feet again, let alone get through the long walk to the spot where he would make both his entrance and ultimately his exit. But, utilizing some hidden will power, he did manage to right himself and was surprised to find himself walking toward the end of the street. True, his legs felt like two pillars of cement and his heart beat so loudly he was sure Jesse James could hear it. And true, too, he had no intention of coming back. He was quite certain that when he turned the corner at the far end of the street, he'd find a way to get the hell out of there.

A moment later, his plans went to pot. A barbed wire fence sealed off the area around the corner. There was simply no place to go. Rance peeked out around the corner and saw Jesse coming toward him, a few hundred feet away. "Stunt man," Rance whispered. "Oh, stunt man!"

Then, inexplicably, Rance found himself making the big move around the corner. It was like stepping into an icy shower. But something had given him momentum and he found himself walking down the street. He'd done it a hundred times before, but this was different. Good had always triumphed, because evil had always faced him with one of its arms tied behind its back. He was conscious, too, that he was completely unable to swagger at this moment, and swagger had been one of the hallmarks of Rance McGrew. No one in the business—Wyatt Earp, Paladin, Marshal Dillon— none of them could swagger like Rance McGrew—and he'd had the added handicap of uplifts and extra-high heels.

Through the sweat, the dust, and the blinding sun, Rance could see Jesse getting closer to him. They were perhaps twenty feet apart now. "Go ahead," Jesse invited. "Reach!"

Rance's look was positively dyspeptic. His momentum stopped. He started to back up.

"I'm gonna count to three," Jesse said.

"This is ridiculous," Rance responded, continuing to back off. "It *never* happens this way."

"One . . ." Jesse said incisively.

The sweat poured down Rance McGrew's arms. "In over a hundred episodes," he said plaintively, "Rance McGrew never got shot down—not even nicked."

"Two . . ." Jesse James's voice was a bell tolling.

"I didn't even want to be in this series," Rance said as he backed up against a black horse-drawn hearse. "I wouldn't have even taken it on if it hadn't been for the residuals."

"Three!"

Rance looked briefly over his shoulder to see what had impeded his backward motion, and sweat showered off his face when he saw the hearse.

"The residuals, plus the fact that they used my own name as the central character."

"Reach!" Jesse said. "I mean right now!"

"Oh, my God!" Rance sobbed. "What you're going to do to the youth of America!" Then he half closed his eyes and went grabbing with both hands for the gun in the holster, fully expecting the hot screaming impact of a bullet in his stomach. He heard the gasp of the onlookers and, still fumbling for his gun, he looked up briefly to see Jesse James holding his own six-gun out, pointing straight at him.

Jesse shook his head. "Jus' like I figgered," he said—almost with disappointment. "This guy couldn't outdraw a crayon."

Tears rolled down Rance's face. "Jesse," he said, holding out his hand supplicatingly, his own six-gun now dangling from his finger, "Jesse . . . give me a break . . . Will you give me a break, Jesse?" He sank to his knees, crying softly. "Jesse . . . I'm too young to die, and I've got a mother, Jesse. I've got a sweet little old mother who depends on me for her support." He let his gun fall to the ground, then he pushed it through the dust toward Jesse James. "Here . . . take it—genuine pearl on the handle. It was sent to me by a fan club in the Bronx. Take anything, Jesse—take everything."

Jesse looked at him coldly. "Ya say ya got nominated fer an Emmy? Man—you can't act any better'n ya can draw!"

Rance felt a surge of hope when no bullet plowed through his body. "What about it, Jesse?" he entreated. "Will you give me a break? I'll do anything you say. Anything at all. I mean it—anything. You name it—I'll do it!"

The gun in Jesse's hand was lowered to his side. He stared at Rance thoughtfully. "Anything?" he inquired.

"Name it!"

Jesse looked off reflectively and rubbed his jaw with the back of his hand. "Marshal," he said quietly, "we ain't a long ways off from a bargain." He picked tentatively at his teeth. "I ain't jus' sure exactly what it is that I want—but I'll think about it some."

Rance held his breath. "You mean . . . you mean you're not going to shoot me down?"

Jesse James shook his head. "Nope. But I'll tell ya what I will do. I'll see to it that you're gonna have to play it mighty careful from now on." He made a gesture toward the sky. "We may be stiffs up there—but we're sensitive."

Again he took out the makings, and as he walked back towards his horse he deftly and gracefully fashioned a cigarette. Once he stopped and looked back toward Rance. "I'll think about it some," he said, and lighted the cigarette. "I'll think about it some." And right in front of Rance McGrew's eyes he disappeared.

"Jesse!" Rance screamed. "Jesse—"

"Jesse!" Rance screamed, and the crew looked up, startled.

There was Rance standing at the bar, staring at his reflection in the mirror. Above him he could see the lighting men, and behind his own reflection was that of Sy Blattsburg and the cameraman.

Sy hurried up to him, his face worried. "You all right, Rance?"

"Yeah," Rance answered weakly. "Yeah, I'm all right." Then, looking around, "But where'd you all go?"

The director exchanged a nervous glance with several of the crew. His voice was even more concerned. "Where did we go? We didn't go anywhere, Rance. Nowhere at all, baby. Are you sure you're all right?"

Rance gulped. "Sure . . . sure, I'm fine—I'm just fine."

Sy turned to face the set. "All right," he said. "Let's get back to business now. Scene one hundred thirteen. Jesse's on the floor—"

Rance gave a startled gasp. He almost had to force himself to turn from the bar to where the ersatz Jesse was lying.

"You think he's unconscious," Sy continued, "but he tries to get you in the back. You fall to the floor, turn over with your gun in your hand, let him have it from on your belly."

At this moment there was the loud honk of a Jaguar horn.

"Somebody wants to see you, Mr. McGrew," one of the grips called from outside. "Says he's your agent."

Rance looked bewildered. "My agent?"

Sy Blattsburg closed his eyes and counted slowly to five under his breath. "Look, Rance," he said, a slight tremor in his voice, "I don't know what your chain of command is. So you go out and talk to your agent. Find out what it is that he wants, and what it is that you want, and what it is we can shoot."

Trancelike, Rance walked out of the saloon and stopped dead in his tracks on the top step of the porch. There was his red Jaguar, just as if nothing had happened. Even the steer horns on the front of the hood were a reminder to him of the reality of Rance McGrew, idol of young and old. But standing alongside of the automobile was an apparition. It was the real Jesse James.

He wore Bermuda shorts, an Italian printed silk sport shirt, and a mauve beret. He was rolling his own cigarette but when he'd finished, he stuck it into a four-inch cigarette holder. He took a deep drag, flicked off the ash, then winked at Rance, who stood swaying between numbing fright and oncoming coma.

"Howdy, marshal," Jesse said warmly. "You said '*any-thing*,' so 'anything' is the following: I'm jus' gonna stick around from picture to picture and make sure you don't hurt no more feelin's." He took out the cigarette holder and studied it thoughtfully, then he looked up and smiled. "Now, in this here scene, the guy that plays me don't fire at your back. He's lost a lot of blood and he's weak as tea, but he manages to git up to his feet, knock you through the window, and then make his getaway out the back." He put the cigarette holder between his teeth. "You dig, marshal?"

Rance stared at him wide-eyed. "Knocks *me* through the window? *Rance McGrew?*"

Jesse's eyes narrowed into slits, not unlike the openings in a Mark III tank. His pupils were the business ends of atomic cannons. "You heard me, marshal," he said. "Knocks you through the window and makes his getaway out the back."

Rance heaved a deep sigh, turned, and reentered the saloon.

Jesse could hear the mumble of voices from inside. There was one piercing wail that belonged to Sy Blattsburg, and some jumbled colloquy that sounded like "Areyououtof-yourmothergrabbingmind? JesseJamesdoeswhat?!"

Jesse smiled and deftly plucked the cigarette out of the holder, stamping it under his patent-leather loafers.

Another voice came from inside. "Scene one hundred thirteen—take two."

There was the sound of a scuffle, and then Rance McGrew came through the window in a welter of shattered glass.

Jesse walked over to stand above him, but in the process took a script from the front seat of the Jag. "I was readin' next week's episode, marshal. The one where ya knock a gun outta Frank James' hand from a fourth-story window half a block away, usin' the base of a lamp."

Rance slowly and painfully got to his feet. "No good?" he inquired softly.

"Stinks!" said Jesse. "The way I see it, Frank hears ya, whirls around, fires from the hip—knocks the lamp outta your hand."

Jesse opened the car door and motioned Rance inside. Then he walked around to the driver's seat, got in, turned the key, and stepped on the gas. The car zoomed backward three quarters of the way across the street, stopped, and then roared forward.

Jesse's voice could be heard over the sound of the engine. "Now, two weeks from now," the voice said, "I think we oughta give Sam Starr a break. He's a nice fella—awful good to his mother—"

The rest of his voice was drowned out by the engine's roar as the car disappeared down the dusty street.

While nothing is certain except death and taxes—and even these may be somewhat variable—it seems reasonable to conjecture that the range riders up in Cowboy Heaven felt appeased. Jesse James used his mandate well, and from that moment on, Rance McGrew, former phony-baloney, became an upright citizen with a preoccupation with all things involving tradition, truth, and cowboy predecessors.

THE NIGHT OF THE MEEK

IT was Christmas. There was absolutely no question about that. Festive good will filled the air like the smell of maple syrup—sweet, sugary, and thick with insistence. There was one more day to complete Christmas shopping and this item of information was dinned into the minds of the citizenry like a proclamation of impending martial law—"One More Shopping Day until Christmas!" It was the war cry of the big sell, and on this twenty-fourth day of the one-thousand-nine-hundred-and-sixty-first year of our Lord, it served as a warning that just a few hours remained for people to open up their wallets and lay rather tired fingers on dog-eared credit cards.

"One More Shopping Day until Christmas." The words were strung in tinseled lettering across the main floor of Wimbel's Department Store. Mr. Walter Dundee, the floor manager of Wimbel's, glanced at them briefly as he did his rounds up and down the aisles, casting businesslike eyes at the organized mayhem surrounding him.

He was a balding little fellow in his fifties, inclined to paunchiness, but briskly efficient in his movements and attitudes. Mr. Dundee could spot a shoplifter, a bum credit risk, or a grimy little child breaking a mechanical toy—he had an abhorrence of children of all ages—in one single all-pervading glance. He could also spot an ineffectual salesperson just by listening to a couple of sentences of the opening pitch.

Mr. Dundee walked through the aisles of Wimbel's that December 24th, barking out orders, snapping fingers, and generally riding herd on these last few moments of Yuletide humbuggery. He extended watery smiles to harried mothers and their squalling children, and he gave explicit and terse directions to any and all questions as to where merchandise could be found, where rest rooms were located, and the exact times of delivery for all purchases over twenty-five dol-

68

lars, no matter how far out in the suburbs they went. As he walked up the aisles past Ladies Hand Bags, toward the Toy Department, he noted the empty Santa Claus chair. One of his sparse little eyebrows, set at a rakish tilt over a tiny blue eye, shot up in fast-mounting concern. There was a sign over the chair which read, "Santa Claus will return at 6:00 o'clock."

The large clock on the west wall read "6:35." Santa Claus was thirty-five minutes late. An incipient ulcer in Mr. Dundee's well-rounded abdomen did little pincer things to his liver. He belched, and felt anger building up like a small flame suddenly blasted by a bellows. That goddamn Santa Claus was a disgrace to the store. What was his name— Corwin? That goddamn Corwin had been the most undependable store Santa Claus they had ever hired. Only yesterday Dundee had seen him pull out a hip flask and take an unsubtle snort—smack dab in the middle of a Brownie troop. Mr. Dundee had sent him an icy look which froze Corwin in the middle of his tippling.

Mr. Dundee was noted for his icy looks. As a boy, thirty-odd years before at military school, he had become Sergeant Major of the Fourth Form—the only non-athlete ever to achieve this eminence—because of the icy look that he carried with him throughout his professional career. It made up for the fact that he stood five feet four inches tall and had a figure like a coke bottle.

Now he felt frustrated that his rage had no outlet, so he scanned the store until he spotted Miss Wilsie, Ladies Inexpensive Jewelry, primping in front of a mirror. He stalked over to her, pinioned her with his look, and then announced:

"You have nothing better to do, Miss Wilsie? Preparing yourself for a beauty contest? There are customers waiting. Be good enough to attend to them!"

He waited only long enough for the color to drain out of the girl's face as she hurried back to her place behind the counter, then he turned again toward the empty Santa Claus chair and cursed the errant Santa Claus, now thirty-eight minutes late.

Henry Corwin sat at the bar, a moth-eaten Santa Claus outfit engulfing his sparse frame. Discolored whiskers hanging from a rubber band covered his chest like a napkin. His cocky little cap, with the white snowball at the end, hung down over his eyes. He picked up his eighth glass of inexpensive rye, blew the snowball off to one side, and deftly slipped the shot glass toward his mouth, downing the drink in one gulp. He looked up at the clock over the bar mirror and noted that the two hands were close together. Precisely where they were he couldn't tell, but he did feel a sense of time passing. Too much time.

He suddenly noticed his reflection in the mirror and realized that he was not drunk enough, because he still looked like a caricature. The Santa Claus uniform which he had rented from Kaplan's Klassy Costume Rental had seen not only better days but many earlier ones. It was made out of thin cotton, patched and repatched. The color had faded to a kind of ailing pink and the white "fur" trim looked like cotton after a boll weevil assault. The cap was several sizes too small, and was actually a reconverted Shriner's fez with the insignia taken off. The face looking back at him had gentle eyes and a warm smile that was slightly lopsided. It crinkled up at the ends and made you want to smile back.

Corwin was neutral to the face. He rarely took note of it. At this moment he was more concerned with the costume, fingering it and noting considerable lillipop stains, week-old ice-cream spots, and some brand-new holes, sizable enough to reveal the two pillows he had strapped over his union suit. He took his eyes away from the reflection and pointed to his empty glass.

The bartender walked over to him and gestured at the clock. "You told me to tell yuh when it was six-thirty," he announced. "It's six-thirty."

Corwin smiled and nodded. "That's exactly what it is," he agreed.

The bartender picked his teeth. "What happens now? Yuh turn into a reindeer?"

Corwin smiled again. "Would that that were so." He held up his empty glass. "One more, huh?"

The bartender poured him a shot. "That's nine drinks and a sandwich—that's four-eighty."

Corwin took a single five-dollar bill from his pocket and put it on the counter. He started the shot glass toward his mouth. But as he did so, he noticed two little faces staring at him through the frosted glass of the front door. Big eyes looked at him in rapt attention and breath-catching worship —the eyes of every kid who, with the purest faith, had known that there *was* a North Pole, that reindeer *did* land on rooftops, and that miracles *did* come down chimneys. Even kids like this had this faith on grimy One-hundred-and-eighteenth street, where Puerto Ricans crowded into cold dirty rooms to gradually realize that poverty wore the same clothes both on lush islands and in concrete canyons a thousand miles away.

Corwin had to stare back at the little faces, and then he had to smile. They looked like slightly soiled cherubs on some creased and aged Christmas card. They were excited that the man in the red suit was looking at them.

Corwin turned his back to them, and quickly gulped the contents of the shot glass. He waited a moment, then looked at the door again. The two little noses pressed against the glass suddenly disappeared. But before they went they waved to Santa Claus at the bar and Corwin waved back.

He looked thoughtfully at the empty shot glass.

"Why do you suppose there isn't really a Santa Claus?" he asked, speaking partly to the glass, partly to the bartender.

The bartender looked up tiredly from drying glasses. "How's that?" he asked.

"Why isn't there a *real* Santa Claus"—Corwin nodded toward the front door—"for kids like that?"

The bartender shrugged. "What the hell am I, Corwin—a philosopher?" He stared at Corwin for a long moment. "Do you know what your trouble is?" he said. "Yuh let that dopey red suit go to your head!"

He picked up the five-dollar bill, rang up the cash register, then put the change in front of Corwin.

Corwin looked at the coins and smiled a little crookedly. "Flip yuh—double or nothing."

"What the hell do yuh think this is, Corwin—Monte Carlo? Go on—get outta here!"

Corwin rose somewhat unsteadily, testing soggy legs. Then, satisfied that they were serviceable, he walked across the room to the front door and out into the cold, snowy night, buttoning the top button of his thin cotton jacket, squeezing his cap down as far as it would go. He put his head into an icy wind and started across the street.

A big Caddie, with a Christmas tree protruding from the trunk, shot past him, honking. A red-faced, angry chauffeur shouted something as the car sped away. Corwin just smiled and went on, feeling the wet flakes cool on his hot face. He stumbled on the opposite curb and reached for the lamppost which was several feet away.

His arms encircled nothing but snowflakes and he pitched forward on his face, landing on a pile of snow next to a garbage can. With great difficulty he got to a sitting position, and became suddenly aware of four ragged little legs standing close by. He looked up to see the two scrawny Puerto Rican kids staring down at him, their little faces dark against the snow.

"Santa Claus," the little girl said, catching her breath, "I want a dolly and a play house."

The silent little boy alongside nudged her with an elbow.

"And a gun," she continued hurriedly, "and a set of soldiers and a fort and a bicycle—"

Corwin looked up into their faces. Even their excitement, their exuberance, the universal Christmas look of all children, couldn't hide the thinness of their faces—nor could the sweetness of them, and the gentleness, hide the fact that their coats were too small for them and not nearly heavy enough for the weather.

Then Henry Corwin began to cry. Alcohol had unlocked all the gates to his reserve—what flooded out of him were the frustrations, the miseries, the failures of twenty years; the pain of the yearly Santa Claus stints in moth-eaten costumes, giving away fantasies that he didn't own, imitating that which was only make-believe to begin with.

Henry Corwin reached out and pulled the children to him, burying his face first against one and then the other, the tears cascading down his cheeks, impossible to stop.

The two little children stared at him—incredulous that this red-coated god, who dealt in toys and unbelievable wonders, could sit on a snowy curb and cry just as they did.

"Por que Santa Claus ésta llorando?" the girl whispered to the little boy.

He answered her in English. "I don't know why he's crying. Maybe we have hurt his feelings."

They watched him for a while until his sobs subsided and he released them, stumbling to his feet and heading down the street away from them—this thin shabby man with the wet face, looking as if he believed that all the anguish of the world was of his doing.

An hour later when Mr. Dundee saw Corwin come in through the side door, he felt that perverse pleasure that is one of the parts built into mean men. Here was someone he could vent his wrath on—a wrath that at this moment was anointed with inflammable oil. He waited for Corwin to walk toward him, drumming his fingertips together behind his back and then deftly grabbing the Santa Claus by the arm as he walked past.

"Corwin," Dundee said through clenched teeth, "you're

almost two hours late! Now get over there and see if you can keep from disillusioning a lot of kids that not only there *isn't* a Santa Claus—but that the one in the store happens to be a bar-hopping clod who'd be more at home playing Rudolph the Red-Nosed Reindeer!" He gave Corwin a shove. "Now get with it—Santa Claus!" This last was spat out like an epithet.

Henry Corwin smiled wanly and started toward the Santa Claus section. He paused by the electric trains and watched two little colored boys staring at them as if they were a collection of miracles. Henry winked at them, went to the control panel, and started to push buttons.

Three trains started up simultaneously, racing around the tracks, over bridges, through tunnels, past station platforms. Little men came out and waved lanterns or threw mail sacks, or did any one of a dozen marvelous things that toy trainmen do. But after a moment it seemed evident that Henry Corwin was not mechanically minded. The two little boys looked at each other with growing concern as a Union Pacific Flyer raced down the tracks on a collision course with a Civil War supply train.

Henry Corwin hastily pushed a few more buttons, but the collision was inevitable. The two trains met head-on in a welter of dented metal, ripped tracks, and flying toy trainmen.

Never one to leave well enough alone, Corwin pushed two more buttons which made the damage total. He switched another set of tracks that sent the heavily laden freight train piling into the wreckage of the first two. Toy trains flew through the air, bridges collapsed; and when the noise had subsided, Corwin saw the two little boys staring at him.

"What do yuh think?" Corwin asked them, smiling a little sheepishly.

The first little boy looked at his companion, then back toward Corwin. "How are yuh on erector sets?" he asked.

Corwin shook his head a little sadly. "About the same."

He tousled the two little heads, and then climbed over the velvet rope that was strung around the Santa Claus chair.

There was a line of waiting children and clock-watching mothers and they surged forward when the slightly moth-eaten Kris Kringle mounted his throne. He sat there for a moment, shutting his eyes briefly as he felt the room start to spin around him. Christmas decorations and colored lights whirled round and round as if he were riding a merry-go-round. He tried to focus on the faces of the children as they kept streaming past him; tried to smile and wave at them. He shut his eyes again, feeling nausea rising inside of him. This time, when he opened them he was face to face with the blurred image of a small gargoyle being pushed toward him by a bosomy, loud woman with a set of shoulders like Tony Galento's.

"Go ahead, Willie," the woman's voice screeched, "climb up on his lap. He won't hurt you, will you, Santa Claus? You go ahead, Willie, you tell him—" She gave the seven-year-old another insistent push toward Santa Claus. Corwin half rose, weaving unsteadily and extending a wavering hand.

"What's your name, little boy?" Corwin asked, and then hiccoughed loudly. He tilted sideways, grabbed for the arm of the chair, and then pitched forward to land on the floor at the little boy's feet. He sat there smiling a little wanly, unable to get up or to do anything else.

The small gargoyle took one look at Corwin and in a blaring voice, similar in pitch to his mother's, shrieked, "Hey, ma! Santa Claus is loaded!"

The gargoyle's mother immediately screamed, "You've got some nerve! You ought to be ashamed!"

Corwin just sat there and shook his head back and forth. "Madam," he said very quietly, "I *am* ashamed."

"Come on, Willie." She grabbed the boy by the arm. "I hope this isn't going to be a traumatic experience for you." She looked over her shoulder toward Corwin. "Sot!"

People, hearing the tone, stopped and stared.

Mr. Dundee hurried up the aisle toward Toyland. He gave an all-pervading glance, and then his voice assumed that unctuous, placating quality of every hard-pressed floor manager.

"Is there some trouble here, madam?"

"Trouble!" the big woman spat back. "No, there's no trouble, except this is the last time I trade in this store. You hire your Santa Clauses out of the gutter!"

She pointed toward Corwin, who was struggling to his feet. He took a hesitant step toward one of the brass poles flanking the entrance to his "throne."

"Madam," he said very gently, "please. It's Christmas."

Willie's mother's face twisted, and in the light of an illuminated sign which read, "Peace on Earth—Good Will to Men," she looked like a cross between the Wicked Witch of the North and a female Ebenezer Scrooge.

"Don't rub it in," she said tersely. "Come on, Willie."

She barged into two people, pushed them bodily out of the way, and dragged the child down the aisle.

Dundee turned to stare toward Corwin, then at the salespeople and customers who had congregated. "All right!" he said grimly. "Back to work! Back to your positions."

He walked toward Corwin, stopping by the velvet rope. His thin lips twitched as he waggled a finger at Corwin and waited for him to come over to him.

"Yes, Mr. Dundee?"

"Simply this," Dundee said, "Mr. Kris Kringle of the lower depths. Since we are only one hour and thirteen minutes away from closing, it is my distinct pleasure to inform you that there is no more need for your services. In other words, you've had it. Now get out of here!"

He turned to face the row of mothers and children, smiling beatifically. "All right, kiddies," he gushed, "free lollipops! Just go over there to the candy counter. Go right ahead!"

He smiled, winked, and looked benevolent as the disappointed children and the hard-pressed mothers moved away from the Santa Claus with the sagging shoulders.

Corwin stared down at the floor, feeling the looks of the children, and after a moment turned and started to walk toward the employees' locker.

"A word of advice," Dundee said to him as he passed. "You'd best get that beat-up red suit back to whatever place you rented it from, before you really tie one on and ruin it for good and all."

Corwin stopped and stared into the twitching angry little face. "Thank you ever so much, Mr. Dundee," he said quietly. "As to my drinking—that is indefensible and you have my abject apologies. I find of late that I have very little choice in the matter of expressing emotions. I can either drink . . . or I can weep. And drinking is so much more subtle."

He paused and looked briefly at the empty Santa Claus chair. "But as for my insubordination"—he shook his head— "I was not rude to that fat woman. I was merely trying to remind her that Christmas isn't just barging up and down department store aisles and pushing people out of the way and screaming 'foul' because she has to open up a purse. I was only trying to tell her that Christmas is something quite different from that. It's richer and finer and truer and . . . and it should allow for patience and love and charity and compassion." He looked into the frozen mask that was Mr. Dundee's face. "That's all I would've told her," he added gently, "had she given me the chance."

"How philosophical!" Mr. Dundee retorted icily. "And as your parting word—perhaps you can tell us how we go about living up to these wonderous Yule standards which you have so graciously and unselfishly laid down for us?"

There was no smile on Corwin's face. He shook his head and shrugged his narrow shoulders. "I don't know how to tell you," he said quietly. "I don't know how at all. All I know is that I'm a defeated, aging, purposeless relic of another time. That I live in a dirty rooming house on a street that's loaded with kids who think that Christmas is a day to stay out of school and nothing more. My street, Mr. Dundee, is full of shabby people where the only thing to come down the chimney on Christmas Eve is more poverty." He smiled crookedly and looked down at his baggy red jacket. "That's another reason I drink. So that when I walk past the tenements I'll think that they're the North Pole and the children are elves, and that I'm really Santa Claus carrying a bag of wonderous things for all of them."

He fingered the worn cotton "fur" around his neck. "I wish, Mr. Dundee," he said as he started to turn away, "I wish that on just one Christmas . . . only one . . . I could see some of the have-nots, the shabby ones, the hopeless and the dreamless ones . . . just on one Christmas . . . I'd like to see the meek inherit the earth."

The crooked smile came again as he looked down at his bony hands and then up at Mr. Dundee. "That's why I drink, Mr. Dundee, and that's why I weep."

He took a deep breath, the strangely twisted little smile still on his face, then turned and shuffled down the aisle past the whispering salesgirls and the tired shoppers, who looked at this symbol of Christmas who was so much more tired than they.

Henry Corwin walked down the avenue past 104th Street. He felt the cold snow on his face and looked vaguely at the festive windows of the stores as he passed. When he reached his block he headed toward the saloon, walking very slowly, hands buried in his armpits. He turned a corner and headed down an alley toward the rear door of the bar, and it was then that he heard the sound.

It was a strange sound. Sleigh bells—or something like them. But very odd. Somehow muffled and indistinct. He stopped and looked skyward. Then he smiled to himself and shook his head, assuring himself that sleigh bells or anything else could be found only in his mind—that tired, whiskey-dulled brain. But after a moment he heard the bells again, this time more persistent and louder.

Corwin had stopped near a loading platform of a wholesale meat plant. He looked up at the sky again and wondered. He started at the caterwauling dissonance of a night-prowling cat that suddenly leaped out from behind a barrel and scurried past him in the snow. It raced across the alley to another loading platform on the other side, leaping to the top of a garbage can and in the process knocking over a burlap bag that rested precariously on top of it. Then the cat disappeared in the darkness.

The burlap bag landed at Corwin's feet and spilled open, depositing half a dozen dented tin cans in the snow. Corwin reached down and righted the bag, shoving the cans back inside. Then he lifted the burlap bag over his shoulder and started to carry it back to the platform. Halfway there he heard the bells again. This time much clearer and very much nearer.

Again he stopped in his tracks and stared up toward the sky, wide-eyed. Another sound joined that of the bells. Corwin couldn't describe it except to make a mental note that it was like the sound of tiny hoofbeats. He very slowly let the burlap bag drop from his shoulders, and once again it fell over and spilled its contents on the ground. Corwin looked down at it, blinked his eyes, rubbed them, and stared.

Protruding from the open bag was the front end of a toy truck, an arm and a leg of a doll, and evidence of other toys of every description. He fell to his knees and started to reach into the bag, taking out truck, doll, play house, a box marked "Electric Train," and then stopped, realizing that the bag must be filled with all such things. He let out a cry of surprise and jammed the toys back in the bag. He hoisted it to his shoulder and started a slow, stumbling trot toward the street, occasionally stopping to pick up a toy that fell, but feeling the words bubbling up inside of him and finally coming out.

"Hey," he shouted as he turned the corner onto 111th Street. "Hey, everybody! Hey, kids—Merry Christmas!"

The 104th Street Mission was a big, ugly, barren place, sullen to the eye and deadening to the spirit. Its main room was a naked square full of straight-backed, uncomfortable benches, with a small platform and organ at the far end.

Large signs dotted the walls with little homilies like, "Love Thy Neighbor," "Do unto Others as You Would Have Others Do unto You," "Faith, Hope and Charity."

Seated up and down the rows of benches were perhaps fifteen shabby old men. A few of them held cheap china mugs filled with watery coffee. They cradled them in cold hands, feeling the warmth and letting the steam rise up into their bearded tired faces. They wore the faces of poverty and age, each encrusted with layer after layer of the hopelessness of lonely old men whose lives had somehow swiftly and silently disintegrated into false teeth, and cheap coffee mugs, and this ugly, drafty room that traded religion and thin gruel in exchange for the last remaining fragments of dignity.

Sister Florence Harvey headed the Mission. After twenty-four years, she had begun to blend with the walls, the benches, and the miserable atmosphere. She was a tall, sour-looking spinster with deep lines imbedded at the corner of her mouth. She pounded the organ with a kind of desperate verve, playing badly but loudly an obscure Christmas carol that had spirit if not melody.

An old man rushed in from the outside and began whispering to another old man who sat on the rear bench. After a moment all the old men were whispering and pointing toward the door. Sister Florence noted the disturbance and tried to drown it out by playing even louder, but by this time some of the men were on their feet, talking loudly and gesturing. Sister Florence finally struck a discordant chord on the organ, rose, and glared at the old men in front of her.

"What's all this about?" she asked angrily. "What's this noise? Why the commotion?"

The old man who had brought the original message took his cap off and rolled it nervously in his hands. "Sister Florence," he said diffidently, "I ain't touched a drop since last Thursday and that's the gospel truth! But I swear to you right now, on account of I seen him with my own eyes— Santa Claus is comin' up the street headin' this way and he's givin' everybody their heart's desire!"

There were mumbled exclamations from the other old men. Dull and saddened eyes turned bright. Tired old faces became animated, and their voices punctuated the room.

"Santa Claus!"

"He's comin' here!"

"And he's bringing us whatever we like!"

The door leading to the street burst open and in walked

Henry Corwin, his face red, his eyes shining, and over his shoulder he carried the bag, brightly wrapped packages protruding from its top.

Corwin put the bag down on the floor, looked up, twinkling, and made a Santa Claus gesture of a finger to nose tip. He looked around the room, smiling—his voice absolutely gurgling with excitement.

"It's Christmas Eve, gentlemen, and I'm in business to make it a merry one." He pointed to one of the old men. "What'll be your pleasure?"

The scrawny little old man pointed to himself, amazed. "Me?" he asked in a toothless wheeze, then he wet his lips. "I fancy a new pipe." He almost held his breath as he said it.

Corwin reached into the bag without even looking. He withdrew a curved Meerschaum. There were "Oh's" and "Ah's" as the old man took the pipe in trembling fingers and stared at it numbly.

Corwin pointed to another old man. "How about you?" he asked.

This little old man opened and closed his mouth several times before a sound came out. "Maybe," he croaked, "maybe a woolen sweater?"

Corwin made a sweeping theatrical gesture. "A woolen sweater you shall have," he trumpeted. He stopped as he reached into the bag and looked up again. "Size?"

The old man held out two thin blue-veined hands. "Who cares?"

Out of the bag came a turtle-neck cashmere, and at this point the old men crowded around Corwin, their frail voices filled with hope.

"Another sweater maybe?"

"How about some pipe tobacco?"

"A carton of cigarettes?"

"New shoes?"

"Smoking jacket?"

And at each request, Corwin produced the desired item by simply reaching into the bag. He was unaware of Sister Florence looking at him angrily from the fringe of the crowd. Finally she pushed her way through to stand over Corwin.

"Now, what's this all about?" she asked acidly. "What's the idea of coming in here and disrupting the Christmas Eve music service?"

Corwin laughed aloud and slapped his hands together. "My dear Sister Florence," he bubbled, "don't ask me to explain.

I can't explain. I'm as much in the dark as everybody else, but I've got a Santa Claus bag here that gives everybody just what they want for Christmas. And as long as it's puttin' out . . . I'm puttin' in!"

His eyes were wet as he reached into the bag again. "How about a new dress, Sister Florence?"

The thin bony woman turned on her heel disapprovingly, but not before she caught a flash of a huge beribboned box that Corwin pulled out of the sack.

Again came the voices of the old men, gentle, plaintive, persistent, and Corwin spent the next five minutes taking things out of the bag, until the room looked like the aftermath of an inventory in a department store.

Corwin was unaware of Sister Florence bringing the policeman in. She pointed to Corwin from the door and the cop made his way over to him. He reached Corwin and hovered over him like a symbol of all the law and order in the world. He put his hand on Corwin's shoulder. "It's Corwin, ain't it?" he asked.

Corwin got to his feet, the grin so broad that his jaw ached. "Henry Corwin, officer," he announced, and then laughed in a spasm of delight. "At least it *was* Henry Corwin. Maybe now it's Santa Claus or Kris Kringle—I don't know."

The policeman regarded him blankly and then sniffed the air. "You're drunk, ain't yuh, Corwin?"

Corwin laughed again and the laugh was so marvelously rich and winning and infectious that all the old men joined in. "Drunk?" Corwin shouted. "Of course I'm drunk! Naturally I'm drunk! I'm drunk with the spirit of Yule! I'm intoxicated with the wonder of Christmas Eve! I'm inebriated with joy and with delight! *Yes, officer—by God, I'm drunk!*"

A toothless old man looked around bewilderedly. "What was them things he was drinking?"

The policeman held up his hands again for quiet and kicked at the burlap bag meaningfully. "We can settle this one in a hurry, Corwin," he said. "You just show me the receipt for all this stuff."

Corwin's smile became frayed at the edges. "The receipt?" he gulped.

"The receipt!"

The old men smiled among themselves, nodded and winked, and turned, smilingly confident, toward Santa Claus.

Corwin didn't nod. He simply swallowed hard and shook his head.

"No receipt, huh?" the policeman asked.

"No receipt," Corwin whispered.

The policeman let out a single snort and kicked at the bag again. "All right," he announced, "collect all the stolen goods and put them in a pile over here. I'll see that they get claimed after I find out where he took the stuff from." He turned to Corwin. "All right, Santa, let's you and me take a little trip down to the precinct." He grabbed Corwin's elbow and started to push him toward the door.

Over his shoulder, Corwin got a last look at the old men. Each was depositing his gift on a pile on the floor. They did it quietly, with no complaints and no sign of disappointment. It was as if they were quite accustomed to miracles being fragile, breakable things. They had spent their lives trying to hold onto illusions, and this was no different.

Sister Florence went back to the platform and shouted out the name of the next carol. "A one, a two, a three," she screeched, and then gave mortal combat to the music while the old men began to sing in sad, cracked little voices. Every now and then one of them would cast a wishful look over his shoulder at a Meerschaum pipe or a cashmere sweater on the pile of gifts that sat a million miles away from them.

In the small detention room at the station house, Officer Flaherty guarded the burlap bag and his prisoner, who sat despondently on a bench, his eyes staring at the floor. The brisk footsteps from outside sounded familiar to Corwin. He knew who they belonged to, and sure enough it was Walter Dundee who was ushered into the room.

Dundee wore a look of contented ferocity. He rubbed his hands together briskly, like a happy executioner. "Aah," he murmured, "here he is." He pointed toward Corwin. "And here we are." He made a gesture encompassing the room, and then pointed to the bag. "And there *that* is! And you, Mr. Corwin, my wistful St. Nicholas, are soon going up the river!" He turned toward Officer Flaherty, his voice hopeful. "Do you suppose he could get as much as ten years?"

The officer looked somber. "It don't look good, Corwin," he said. "Of course they might lop off a few months if you was to tell us where the rest of the loot was." He looked at Dundee and jerked his head in Corwin's direction. "He's been givin' away stuff for two and a half hours. He must have a warehouse full of it."

Corwin looked first toward Dundee, then at the policeman, and then at the burlap bag. "I'm glad you brought that up," he said quietly. "There's a little discrepancy here."

Dundee's lips twitched. "Listen, you moth-eaten Robin Hood—the wholesale theft of thousands of dollars' worth of goods is not a 'little discrepancy'!" He moved over to the bag and started to open it. "Though I can tell you right now, Corwin, that this whole affair has come as no surprise to me! I happen to be a practical judge of human nature."

He dipped into the bag and started to remove things—garbage bags, tin cans, broken bottles, and a large black cat that leaped out, squalling, and ran out of the room.

"I perceived that criminal glint in your eyes," Dundee continued, as he wiped some catsup off his cuff, "the very first moment I laid eyes on you! I'm not a student of human misbehavior for nothing. And I can assure you—"

Suddenly, Dundee stopped talking and gaped at the pile of garbage he had heaped on the floor. Quite abruptly he realized what he had been removing. He stared at the bag, incredulous. Officer Flaherty did the same.

Corwin smiled ever so slightly. He waggled a finger at the bag. "Mr. Dundee," he said softly, "you've kind of put your finger on the problem!" He waggled his finger at the bag again. "It can't seem to make up its mind whether to give out garbage or gifts."

Flaherty's face turned white and his mouth worked before any sound came out. "Well . . . well . . ." he spluttered, "it was givin' out gifts when I seen it." He turned to Dundee. "Whatever they wanted, Corwin was supplying it, and it wasn't tin cans neither! It was gifts. Toys. All kinds of expensive stuff. You might as well admit it, Corwin."

Corwin smiled. "Oh, I admit it all right. When I put in—it put out." He scratched his jaw thoughtfully. "But I believe the essence of our problem here is that we're dealing with a most unusual bag—"

Dundee waved him quiet. "My advice to you, Corwin, is to clean this mess up and get out of here."

Corwin shrugged, went over to the bag, and started to put the debris back inside.

In the meantime Dundee turned to the policeman. "And you, Officer Flaherty," he said devastatingly, "call yourself a policeman! Well, I suppose it's a demanding task to distinguish between a bag full of garbage and an inventory of expensive stolen gifts."

The policeman's lower lip sagged. "You can believe me, Mr. Dundee," he said plaintively, "it's just like Corwin says—

we're dealing with somethin' . . . somethin' supernatural here."

Dundee shook his head. "You know . . . you amaze me, Officer Flaherty. You really amaze me. In other words, all we need to do is ask Mr. Corwin to make a little abracadabra for us and no sooner said—done!" He looked up toward the ceiling. "Well, go ahead, Corwin. I fancy a bottle of cherry brandy, vintage nineteen-O-three." He threw up his hands in disgust and shut his eyes.

Corwin was halfway to the door. He paused, smiled a little thoughtfully, and then nodded. "Nineteen-O-three. A good year." He reached into the bag for a gift-wrapped package which he placed on the bench. Then he hoisted the bag over his shoulder and walked out of the room.

Dundee opened his eyes, took out a cigar, pointed it at the policeman. "Now, as for you, Officer Flah—" He stopped abruptly, staring at the beribboned box on the bench.

The policeman walked over to it and with shaking fingers pulled out a large bottle—a gift card hanging from it. His voice wavered slightly as he read it aloud. "Merry Christmas, Mr. Dundee."

The cork suddenly and inexplicably popped out of the bottle, and the policeman sat down on the bench because his legs could no longer support him.

Dundee's mouth was wide open as he stared at the bottle.

The policeman finally picked it up, wiped the neck, and held it out. "After you, Mr. Dundee."

Dundee took a couple of shaky steps over to Flaherty. He accepted the bottle and tilted it to his mouth, then he handed it back to the policeman. The two men sat side by side taking turns, doing honors to an odd-ball gift that they were both sure was a figment of their imagination, just the sudden warm feeling in their stomachs must also be illusory. But sat there they did. And drink they did. And the make-believe liquid in the imaginary bottle was the best-tasting brandy they'd ever had.

A light snow drifted gently down through the glow of a street corner lamp where Henry Corwin sat, the burlap bag between his legs. People came and went. But they came empty-handed and left with whatever precious little thing they had asked for. An old man carried a smoking jacket. A sad-faced immigrant woman in a shawl gazed lovingly at furlined boots that she craddled in her arms as she walked away. Two little Puerto Rican children loaded their gifts onto a brand-new red wagon and, chattering like bright-eyed squirrels, ran through the snow. A rheumy-eyed Bowery bum clutched happily at a portable television set. And still people came and went—a tiny Negro girl, barely able to walk, an eighty-year-old ex-First Mate from a banana boat that hadn't sailed in twenty years, a blind gospel singer who stared, unseeing, into the snow-filled night, crying softly as two of his neighbors helped pull a new organ down the sidewalk toward his tenement room.

And Henry Corwin's voice carried over the traffic noise and his hands flew in and out of the bag. "Merry Christmas . . . Merry Christmas . . . Merry Christmas . . . Here's a sweater for you. What's that, darling—a toy? Here you are. An electric train? Got lots of them. Smoking jackets? Lots of them here. What do you want, sweetheart—a dolly? What color hair would you like, darlin' . . . blonde, brunette, red, or what have you?"

And still the gifts came, and Henry Corwin felt a joy, a fulfillment, a sense of contentment he had never before known. It was when bells on a distant church steeple rang out midnight that Henry Corwin realized that most of the people had disappeared and that the bag was empty burlap lying limply at his feet.

The toothless little old man with his smoking jacket worn over his shabby coat looked off in the direction of the chimes. "It's Christmas, Henry," he said softly. "Peace on earth, good will to men."

A little Puerto Rican child, setting up toy soldiers in the snow, smiled at Santa Claus sitting on the curb. "God bless us," he whispered, "everyone."

Corwin smiled and felt a wetness on his cheeks that wasn't snow. The smile persisted as he touched the burlap sack. "A Merry Christmas to all." He got to his feet and looked at the old man standing close to him. He straightened the phony beard and started to walk down the street.

The old man touched his arm. "Hey, Santa! Nothin' for *yourself* this Christmas?"

"For myself?" Corwin said quietly. "Why, I've had the nicest Christmas since the beginning of time."

"But with nothin' for yourself?" the old man persisted. He pointed to the empty bag. "Not a thing?"

Corwin touched his make-believe whiskers. "Do you know something? I can't think of anything I want." He looked toward the empty bag. "I think the only thing I've *ever* wanted was to be the biggest gift-giver of all times. And in a way I've had that tonight." He walked slowly along the snowy sidewalk. "Though if I did have a choice . . . any choice at all . . . of a gift"—he paused and looked back toward the old man—"I guess I'd wish I could do this every year." He winked and grinned. "Now, that *would* be a gift, wouldn't it!"

The old man smiled back at him.

"God bless you," Corwin said, "and a Merry Christmas."

"To you, Henry," the old man said, "to you."

Henry Corwin walked slowly down the street, feeling a sudden emptiness—a dullness, as if he had traveled through a land of lights only to enter suddenly a gray limbo. He didn't know why he stopped, but then he realized he was standing at the entrance of the alley. He looked into it and, double-taking, looked in again and caught his breath. All his brain, his logic, his understanding of what could and couldn't exist told him in this one flashing instant that this was simply an illusion added to a night full of illusions. But there it was.

Set back deep at the far end of the alley was a sleigh and eight diminutive reindeer. And even more incredible, there was a tiny pipe-smoking elf standing alongside.

Corwin jammed his knuckles into his eyes and rubbed hard, but when he peeked through his fingers there was the scene just as he'd seen it.

"We've been waiting quite a while, Santa Claus," the elf said, taking a puff of his pipe.

Corwin shook his head. He wanted just to lie down in the snow and go to sleep. The whole thing was make-believe—of this there could be no doubt. He smiled foolishly and then giggled as he pointed to the pipe. "That'll stunt your growth." Then he giggled again and decided there was no point in going to sleep, since obviously that's precisely what he *was*—asleep.

The little elf's voice carried with it just a tinge of impatience. "Did you hear me? I said we've been waiting quite a while, Santa Claus."

Corwin let it sink in and then very slowly raised his right hand and pointed to himself.

The elf nodded. "We've got a year of hard work ahead of us to prepare for *next* Christmas, so come on awready!"

Henry Corwin walked slowly into the alley and, as if in a dream, mounted into the tiny sleigh.

Officer Patrick J. Flaherty and Walter Dundee walked down the steps of the station house arm and arm, feeling no pain at all. They stopped at the foot of the steps.

"Going home now, Officer Flaherty?" Dundee asked.

Flaherty smiled happily back at him through glazed eyes. "Goin' home, Mr. Dundee. And you?"

"Going home, Officer Flaherty. This is quite the nicest Christmas Eve I've ever had."

There was a sound and both men looked up into the night sky.

Dundee shivered. "Flah . . . Flah . . . Flaherty? I could have sworn that—" He looked at the policeman, who was blinking and rubbing his eyes. "Did *you* see it?"

The policeman nodded. "I thought I did."

"What *did* you see?

"Mr. Dundee—I don't think I'd better tell you. You'd report me for drinking on duty."

"Go ahead," Dundee insisted. *"What did you see?"*

"Mr. Dundee . . . it was Corwin! Big as life . . . in a sleigh with reindeer . . . sittin' alongside an elf and headin' up toward the sky!" He closed his eyes and heaved a tremendous sigh. "That's about the size of it, ain't it, Mr. Dundee?"

Dundee nodded. "That's about the size of it, Officer Flaherty." His voice sounded small and strained. He turned to the big cop. "I'll tell you something. You'd better come home with me. We'll brew up some hot coffee and we'll pour some whiskey into it, and we'll . . ." His voice drifted off as he stared toward the snow-filled sky, and when he looked back at Flaherty he wore a smile that somehow shone. "And we'll thank God for miracles, Officer Flaherty. That's what we'll do. We'll thank God for miracles."

Arm and arm, the two men walked off into the night—and over the disappearing sound of tiny bells came the deep resonant ringing of the church bells as they ushered in the next day. The wondrous day. The joyous day above all joyous days—the day of Christmas.

THE
MIDNIGHT
SUN

"THE secret of a successful artist," an old instructor had told her years ago, "is not just to put paint on canvas—it is to transfer emotion, using oils and brush as a kind of nerve conduit."

Norma Smith looked out of the window at the giant sun and then back to the canvas on the easel she had set up close to the window. She had tried to paint the sun and she had captured some of it physically—the vast yellow-white orb which seemed to cover half the sky. And already its imperfect edges could be defined. It was rimmed by massive flames in motion. This motion was on her canvas, but the heat—the incredible, broiling heat that came in waves and baked the city outside—could not be painted, nor could it be described. It bore no relation to any known quantity. It simply had no precedent. It was a prolonged, increasing, and deadening fever that traveled the streets like an invisible fire.

The girl put the paint brush down and went slowly across the room to a small refrigerator. She got out a milk bottle full of water and carefully measured some into a glass. She took one swallow and felt its coolness move through her. For the past week just the simple act of drinking carried with it very special reactions. She couldn't remember actually *feeling* water before. Before, it had simply been thirst and then alleviation; but now the mere swallow of anything cool was an experience by itself. She put the bottle back inside the refrigerator and looked briefly at the clock on the bookcase. It read "11:45." She heard footsteps coming down the stairs outside and she walked slowly over to the door, opened it, and went out into the hall.

A little four-year-old girl stared up at her soberly, her eyes fixed on Norma's glass of water. Norma knelt down and put the glass to the child's lips.

"Susie!" a man's voice cut in. "Don't take the lady's water."

Norma looked up at a tall, sweat-drenched man in an un-buttoned sport shirt. "That's all right, Mr. Schuster," Norma said, "I have plenty."

"Nobody has plenty," the man said as he reached the bottom of the stairs and moved the little girl aside. "There's no such thing as 'plenty' any more." He took the little girl's hand and crossed the hall to knock on the opposite door. "Mrs. Bronson," he called, "we're leaving now."

Mrs. Bronson opened the door and stepped out. She was a middle-aged woman in a thin housecoat, her face gleaming with sweat. She looked frowsy and dumpy, although Norma could recollect that she had been a petite, rather pretty woman not too long ago—much younger-looking than her years. Now her face was tired, her hair stringy and un-kempt.

"Did you get gas?" Mrs. Bronson inquired in a flat, tired voice.

The tall man nodded. "I got twelve gallons. I figured that'd take us at least to Buffalo."

"Where are you going?" Norma asked.

The tall man's wife came down the stairs. "We're trying to get to Toronto," she said. "Mr. Schuster has a cousin there."

Mrs. Bronson reached down to stroke the little girl's hair, and then wiped some of the perspiration from the tiny flushed face. "I'm not sure it's wise—you trying to do this. The highways are packed. Bumper to bumper, the radio said. Even with the gas shortage and everything—"

Schuster cut her off. "I know that," he said tersely, "but we gotta try anyway." He wet his lips. "We just wanted to say good-bye to you, Mrs. Bronson. We've enjoyed living here. You've been real kind." Then, somehow embarrassed, he turned quickly to his wife. "Let's go, honey." He picked up the single suitcase and, holding his little daughter's hand, started down the steps. His wife followed.

"Good luck," Mrs. Bronson called down to them. "Safe trip."

"Good-bye, Mrs. Bronson," the woman's voice called back.

The front door opened and closed. Mrs. Bronson stared down the steps for a long moment, then turned to Norma. "And now we are two," she said softly.

"They were the last?" Norma asked, pointing to the steps.

"The last. Building's empty now except for you and me."

A man, carrying a tool kit, came out of Mrs. Bronson's apartment.

"She's runnin' again, Mrs. Bronson," he said. "I wouldn't sign no guarantee as to how long she'll run—but she shouldn't give yuh any trouble for a while." He looked briefly at Norma and fingered his tool kit nervously. "Was you gonna pay for this in cash?" he asked.

"I have a charge account," Mrs. Bronson said.

The repairman was ill at ease. "Boss said I should start collectin' in cash." He looked a little apologetically toward Norma. "We been workin' around the clock. Refrigerators breakin' down every minute and a half. Everybody and his brother tryin' to make ice—then with the current bein' cut off every coupla hours, it's tough on the machines." With obvious effort he looked back at Mrs. Bronson. "About that bill, Mrs. Bronson—"

"How much is it?"

The repairman looked down at his tool kit; his voice was low. "I gotta charge yuh a hundred dollars." He just shook his head disconsolately.

The quiet of Mrs. Bronson's voice did not cover her dismay. "A hundred dollars? For fifteen minutes' work?"

The repairman nodded miserably. "For fifteen minutes' work. Most outfits are chargin' double that, and even triple. It's been that way for a month. Ever since . . ." He looked out the hall window toward the street. "Ever since the thing happened."

There was an embarrassing silence and finally Mrs. Bronson took off her wedding ring. "I don't have any money left," she said quietly, "but this is gold. It's worth a lot." She held the ring out to him.

The repairman failed to meet her eyes. He made a jerky spasmodic motion that was neither acceptance nor rejection. Then he looked at the ring and shook his head. "Go ahead and charge it," he said, keeping his face averted; "I ain't takin' a lady's weddin' ring." He went over to the stairs. "Good-bye, Mrs. Bronson. Good luck to you." He paused at the top of the stairs.

The yellow-white sun was framed in the window above him. It was constant now, but somehow an evil thing that could no longer be ignored.

"I'm gonna try to get my family out tonight," the repairman said, staring out the window. "Drivin' north. Canada, if we can make it. They say it's cooler there." He turned to look back toward the two women. "Not that it makes much difference—just kind of . . . kind of prolonging it." He smiled, but it was a twisted smile. "Like everybody rushin' to fix their refrigerators and air conditioners . . ." He shook his head. "It's nuts. It's just prolonging it, that's all."

He started slowly down the steps, his big shoulders slumped. "Oh, Christ!" they heard him say as he turned at the landing and went down again. "Christ, it's hot!" His footsteps crossed the downstairs hall.

Norma leaned against the side of the door. "What happens now?" she asked.

Mrs. Bronson shrugged. "I don't know. I heard on the radio that they'd only turn the water on for an hour a day from now on. They said they'd announce what time." She suddenly stared at Norma. "Aren't you going to leave?" she blurted.

Norma shook her head. "No, I'm not going to leave." She forced a smile, then turned and went back into her apartment, leaving the door open.

Mrs. Bronson followed her. Norma walked over to the window. The sun bathed her with its heat and with its strange, almost malevolent light. It had changed the entire city. The streets, the buildings, the stores had taken on a sickly oyster color. The air was heavy and soggy.

Norma felt perspiration rolling down her back and her legs. "I keep getting this crazy thought," she said, "this crazy thought that I'll wake up and none of this will have happened. I'll wake up in a cool bed and it'll be night outside and there'll be a wind and there'll be branches rustling —shadows on the sidewalk, a moon."

She turned her face to stare directly out of the window and it was like standing in front of an open oven. The waves of heat struck at her, pushed into her flesh, poured through her pores. "And traffic noises," she continued in a softer voice, "automobiles, garbage cans, milk bottles, voices." She raised her hand and pulled at the cord of the venetian blind. The slats closed and the room became shadowed but the heat remained. Norma closed her eyes. "Isn't it odd . . ." she said, reflectively, ". . . isn't it odd the things we took for granted . . ." There was a pause. ". . . *while we had them?*"

Mrs. Bronson's hands were like two nervous little birds fluttering. "There was a scientist on the radio," she said, forcing herself to be conversational. "I heard him this morning. He said that it would get a lot hotter. More each day.

Now that we're moving so close to the sun. And that's why we're . . . that's why we're . . ."

Her voice trailed off. She couldn't bring herself to say the word. She didn't want to hear it aloud. The word was "doomed." But unspoken or not, it hung there in the still hot air.

It had been just four and a half weeks ago that the earth had suddenly, inexplicably, changed its eliptical orbit, and had begun to follow a path which gradually, moment by moment, day by day, took it closer to the sun.

Midnight became almost as hot as noon—and almost as light. There was no more darkness, no more night. All of man's little luxuries—the air conditioners, the refrigerators, the electric fans that stirred up the air—they were no longer luxuries. They were pitiful and panicky keys to temporary survival.

New York City was like a giant sick animal slowly mummifying, its juices boiling away. It had emptied itself of its inhabitants. They had trekked north toward Canada in a hopeless race against a sun which had already begun to overtake them. It was a world of heat. Each day the sun appeared larger and larger; and each day heat was added to heat until thermometers boiled over; and breathing, talking, moving, came with agony. It was a world of a perpetual high noon.

It was the next afternoon, and Norma walked up the steps carrying a heavy bag of groceries. A can and some wilted carrots protruded from the top. She stopped on the landing between two floors and caught her breath. Her light cotton dress clung to her like a wet glove.

"Norma?" Mrs. Bronson's voice called out. "Is that you, honey?"

Norma's voice was weak and breathless. "Yes, Mrs. Bronson."

She started up the steps again as the landlady came out of her apartment and looked at the bag in Norma's arms. "The store was open?"

Norma half smiled. "Wide open. I think that's the first time in my life I've been sorry I was born a woman." She put the bag on the floor and pointed to it. "That's all I was strong enough to carry. There weren't any clerks. Just a handful of people taking all they could grab." She smiled again and picked up the bag. "At least we won't starve—and there are three cans of fruit juice on the bottom."

Mrs. Bronson followed her into her apartment. "Fruit juice!" She clapped her hands together like a little child, her voice excited. "Oh, Norma . . . could we open one now?"

Norma turned to her, smiled at her gently, and patted her cheek. "Of course we can."

She started to empty the bag while Mrs. Bronson kept opening and closing drawers in the kitchen area.

"Where is the can opener?"

Norma pointed to the far drawer on the left. "In there, Mrs. Bronson."

The landlady's fingers trembled with excitement as she opened up the drawer, rummaged through its interior, and finally pulled out a can opener. She carried it over to Norma and abruptly grabbed a can out of the girl's hand. And then, her hands shaking, she tried to get the point of the opener firmly into the can, breathing heavily and spasmodically as she did so. Can and opener fell from her fingers and landed on the floor. She dropped to her hands and knees, emitting a childlike wail, and then suddenly bit her lip and closed her eyes.

"Oh, my God!" she whispered. "I'm acting like some kind of an animal. Oh, Norma—I'm so sorry—"

Norma knelt beside her and picked up the can and the opener. "You're acting like a frightened woman," she said quietly. "You should have seen *me* in that store, Mrs. Bronson. Running down the aisles. I mean, *running*. This way and that way, knocking over things, grabbing and throwing away, then grabbing again." She smiled and shook her head, and then got to her feet. "And at that," she continued, "I think I was the calmest person in the store. One woman just stood in the center of the room and cried. Just cried like a baby. Kept pleading for someone to help her." Norma shook her head again, wanting to obliterate the scene from her mind.

A small radio on the coffee table suddenly lit up and began to hum. After a while there came the voice of an announcer. It was deep and resonant, but somehow sounded strange.

"Ladies and gentlemen," the voice said, "this is station WNYG. We are remaining on the air for one hour to bring you traffic advisories and other essential news. First, a bulletin from the Office of Civil Defense. Traffic moving north and east out of New York City—motorists are advised to remain off the highways until further notice. Traffic on the Garden State Parkway, the Merritt Parkway, and the New

York State Throughway heading north is reported bumper to bumper, stretching out in some places to upwards of fifty miles. Please . . . remain off the highways until further notice."

There was a pause and the voice took on a different tone. "And now today's weather report from the Director of Meteorology. The temperature at eleven o'clock Eastern Standard Time was one hundred and seventeen degrees. Humidity ninety-seven per cent. Barometer steady. Forecast for tomorrow . . ." Another pause, and the tone changed again. "Forecast for tomorrow . . ." There was a long silence as Norma and Mrs. Bronson stared toward the radio. Then the announcer's voice came on once more. "Hot. More of the same, only hotter."

The sound of whispered voices came from the radio. "I don't care," the announcer said clearly. "Who the hell do they think they're kidding with this weather report crap? . . . Ladies and gentlemen," he went on, a strange kind of laughter in his voice, "tomorrow you can fry eggs on sidewalks, heat up soup in the ocean, and get yourselves the sunburn of your lives just by standing in the goddamn shade!" This time the whispered voices were more urgent and intense, and the announcer was obviously reacting to them. "What do you mean, panic!" he blurted out. "Who the hell is there left to panic?" There came the sound of grim laughter.

"Ladies and gentlemen," the voice continued, "I'm told that my departing from the script might panic you. It happens to be my contention that there aren't a dozen of you left in this city who are listening to me. I'm starting a special contest now. Anyone within sound of my voice can tear off the top of their thermometer and send it to me. I'll send them my own specially devised booklet on how to stay warm when the sun is out at midnight. Now maybe I can find a couple of real pizazz commercials for you. How about a nice cold beer? Wouldn't that taste just great?" The voice faded off slightly. "Lemme alone," it said, "do you hear me? Goddamn it, lemme alone! Let go of me!" More frantic whisperings followed, and then a dead silence, finally replaced by the sound of a needle scratching on a record and then the sound of dance music.

Norma and Mrs. Bronson exchanged a look.

"You see?" Norma said, as she started to open up the can of grapefruit juice. "You're not the only frightened one."

She unbuttoned the top buttons of her dress, then took two glasses down from a shelf and poured the juice into them. She handed one of the glasses to Mrs. Bronson, who looked at it but didn't drink.

"Go ahead, Mrs. Bronson," Norma said softly, "it's grapefruit juice."

The older woman looked down at the floor, and very slowly put the glass down on the counter ."I can't," she said. "I can't just live off you, Norma. You'll need this yourself."

Norma moved over to her swiftly and held her tightly by her shoulders. "We're going to have to start living off of each other, Mrs. Bronson." She picked up the glass and handed it to the landlady, then winked at her and held up her own glass. "Here's looking at you."

Mrs. Bronson made a valiant attempt at a smile and a wink of her own, but as she put the glass to her lips she had to stifle a sob, and almost gagged as she swallowed.

The music on the radio went off abruptly, and a small electric fan at the end of the room stopped its desultory movement to left and right, the blades coming to a halt like some tired, aged airplane.

"The current's off again," Norma said quietly.

Mrs. Bronson nodded. "Every day it stays on for a shorter time. What if . . ." she began, and she turned away.

"What?" Norma asked softly.

"What if it shuts off and doesn't come back on again? It would be like an oven in here—as hot as it is now, as unbearable, it would be so much worse." She put her hands to her mouth. "Norma, it would be so much worse."

Norma didn't answer her. Mrs. Bronson drank a little more of the grapefruit juice and put the glass down. She walked around the room aimlessly, looking at the paintings that lined the room. And there was something so hopeless in the round, perspiring face, the eyes so terribly frightened, that Norma wanted to take her into her arms.

"Norma," Mrs. Bronson said, staring at one of the paintings.

Norma moved closer to her.

"Paint something different today. Paint something like a scene with a waterfall and trees bending in the wind. Paint something . . . paint something cool."

Suddenly her tired face became a mask of anger. She seized the painting, lifted it up, and then threw it down on the floor. "Damn it, Norma!" she screamed. *"Don't paint the sun any more!"* She knelt down and began to cry.

Norma looked at the ripped canvas lying in front of her. It was the painting she'd been working on—a partially finished oil of the street outside, with the hot white sun hovering overhead. The jagged tear across the picture gave it a strangely surrealistic look—something Dali might have done.

The old woman's sobs finally subsided but she stayed on her knees, her head down.

Norma gently touched her shoulder. "Tomorrow," she said softly, "tomorrow I'll try to paint a waterfall."

Mrs. Bronson reached up to take Norma's hand and held on to it tightly. She shook her head; her voice was a hoarse whisper. "Oh, Norma, I'm sorry. My dear child, I'm so sorry. It would be so much better if—"

"If what?"

"If I were to just die." She looked up into Norma's face. "So much better for *you*."

Norma knelt down, cupping the old face in her hands. "Don't ever say that again to me, Mrs. Bronson. For God's sake, don't ever say that again! We need each other now. We need each other desperately."

Mrs. Bronson let her cheek rest on Norma's hand and then slowly got to her feet.

A policeman came up the stairs and appeared at the open door. His shirt was unbuttoned. His sleeves had been cut off and were ragged and uneven at the elbows. He looked from Norma to Mrs. Bronson and wiped the sweat off his sunburned face. "You the only ones in the building?" he asked.

"Just me and Miss Smith," Mrs. Bronson answered.

"You had your radio on lately?" the policeman asked.

"It's on all the time," Mrs. Bronson said, and turned to Norma. "Norma, honey, what station did we—"

The policeman interrupted. "It doesn't make any difference. There're only two or three on the air now and they figure by tomorrow there won't be any. The point is— we've been trying to get a public announcement through for everyone left in the city." He looked from one face to the other and then around the room, obviously reluctant to go on. "There isn't going to be a police force tomorrow. We're disbanding. Over half of us have gone already. A few volunteered to stay back and tell everyone we could that—"

He saw the fear creep in to Mrs. Bronson's face and he tried to make his voice steady. "Best thing would be to keep your doors locked from now on. Every wild man, every crank and maniac around will be roaming the streets. It's not going to be safe, ladies, so keep your doors locked." He looked at them and made a mental note that Norma was the stronger of the two and the more reliable. "You got any weapons in here, miss?" he asked, directing the question to her.

"No," Norma answered, "no, I haven't."

The policeman looked thoughtful for a moment and then unbuckled his holster, removing a police .45. He handed it to Norma. "You better hang onto this. It's loaded." He forced a smile toward the landlady. "Good luck to you."

He turned and started down the steps, Mrs. Bronson following him out. "Officer," she said, her voice shaking, "officer, what's going to happen to us?"

The policeman turned to her from halfway down the steps. His face was tired, drained out. "Don't you know?" he asked quietly. "It's just going to get hotter and hotter, then maybe a couple of days from now"—he shrugged—"four or five at the most, it'll be too hot to stand it." He looked over Mrs. Bronson's shoulder at Norma standing in the door, still holding onto the gun. His mouth was a grim straight line. "Then you use your own judgment, ladies." He turned and continued down the steps.

It was the following day or night. The current had gone off, and with it the clocks, so that the normal measurement of time was no longer operative. A sick white light bathed the streets and chronology had warped with the heat.

Norma lay on the couch in her slip, feeling the waves of heat, like massive woolen blankets piled on top of her. It was as if someone were pushing her into a vat of boiling mud, forcing the stuff into her mouth, her nose, her eyes, gradually immersing her in it. Between the nightmare of sleep and the nightmare of reality, she groaned. After a moment she opened her eyes, feeling a dull, throbbing ache in her temples.

She forced herself to rise from the couch, feeling the same ponderous heaviness as she walked across the room to the refrigerator. She opened the door, took out the milk bottle full of water, and poured herself a quarter of a glass. This she sipped slowly as she retraced her steps across the room to the window. She gasped as her hands touched the sill. It was like touching hot steel. Her fingers went to her mouth and she stood there licking them, and finally she poured a few drops of water from the glass onto them. She listened for sounds, but there was absolute stillness. At last she turned and crossed the room, opened the door, and went out into the hall. She knocked on the door of Mrs. Bronson's apartment.

"Mrs. Bronson?" she called. There was no answer. "Mrs. Bronson?"

There were slow footsteps behind the door and then the sound of a door chain. The door opened a few inches and Mrs. Bronson peered out.

"Are you all right?" Norma asked.

The landlady unhooked the chain and opened the door. Her face looked pinched and ill, her eyes watery and too bright. "I'm all right," she said. "It's been so quiet. I haven't heard a sound." She moved out into the hall and looked over the landing toward the steps. "What time is it?"

Norma glanced at her watch and shook her wrist. "It's stopped. I'm not sure what time it is. I'm not even sure whether it's morning or night."

"I think it's about three o'clock in the afternoon," Mrs. Bronson said. "It feels about three in the afternoon." She shook her head. "I think that's what time it is."

She closed her eyes very tightly. "I lay down for a while," she went on. "I tried shutting the curtains to keep the light out, but it gets so stifling when the curtains are shut." She smiled wanly. "I guess that's psychological, isn't it? I mean, I don't think there's much difference between out there and in here."

From up on the roof came the sound of glass breaking, and then a loud thump.

Mrs. Bronson's hand shot out and grabbed Norma. "What was that?" she whispered.

"Something . . . something fell."

"Oh, no . . . it was *someone*."

Norma looked up the steps leading to the top floor. "Didn't you lock the roof door?" she whispered, feeling a nightmare moving in on her.

"Yes," Mrs. Bronson said hurriedly, then clapped a hand to her mouth. "No," she corrected herself, and shook her head wildly. "I don't know. I don't remember. I thought I did."

A door above them squeaked open and Norma didn't wait to hear any more. She took Mrs. Bronson by the arm and pulled her into her apartment, slamming the door and locking it. The two women barely breathed as the sound of footsteps came down the stairs. They stopped outside.

Mrs. Bronson turned to Norma. Her mouth opened as if

ready to say something, but Norma clamped her hand over it and warned her with her eyes to be silent.

There was the sound of movement in the hall, and footsteps came to the door. "Hey!" a man's voice called out. "Who's in there? Somebody in there?"

Norma felt all the muscles in her body constrict. Neither of them made a sound.

"Come on out," the voice said. "I know you're in there. Come on out and be friendly." The voice sounded impatient. "Come on—I ain't got all day. You come out or I'm gonna come in!"

Norma, her hand still on Mrs. Bronson's mouth, looked desperately around the room. She saw the policeman's gun on the coffee table, moved over, and picked it up. She went to the door and held the gun close to the keyhole. She cocked it and then put her face against the door. "Did you hear that?" she asked in a loud voice. "That was a gun. Now get out of here. Go down the steps and go out the front door. Leave us alone."

Heavy breathing sounded on the other side of the door. Whoever was out there was thinking it over very carefully.

"Okay, honey," the voice finally said. "I never argue with a lady who has a gun."

Shuffling footsteps started down the stairs and Norma moved quickly to the window, craning her neck so that she could see the front steps below. She waited, but no one came out of the building.

"I don't think he went down the stairs—" she started to say, and then, hearing the click of a key, she whirled around to see Mrs. Bronson opening the door. "Mrs. Bronson!" she cried. "Wait a min—"

The door was pushed open and a man stood there—a hulking, heavy-featured giant of a man in a torn undershirt, his face and body grimy. Mrs. Bronson screamed and started to rush past him. He caught her by the arm and threw her aside.

Norma held up the gun, clawing at it, trying to find the trigger. The man lashed out, knocking the gun aside, and backhanded her across the face. Norma was stunned by the jolting pain. The man kicked the gun across the floor, then walked over and put his foot on it. He stood there breathing heavily, looking from one to the other.

"Crazy dames! It's too hot to play games. It's too damn hot!"

He reached down and picked up the gun, then looked

around the room. He saw the refrigerator and went over to it. One bottle of water was left in it and he smiled with relief as he took it out. He threw his head back and drank, the water running out the corners of his mouth and dripping down the front of him. When he had finished the bottle he threw it to one side, where it broke on the floor with incredible loudness.

He walked slowly across the room, still holding the gun, and looked at the pictures, studying them carefully. He looked at Norma and pointed to one of the paintings. "You do this?" he asked.

Norma nodded, not daring to speak.

"You're good," the man said. "You paint real good. My wife used to paint."

The terror overflowed from Mrs. Bronson. "Please," she moaned, "please leave us alone. We didn't do you any harm. Please—"

The man just stared at her as if her voice came from far away. He turned, looked at the painting again and then down at the gun, as if he had suddenly become aware of it. Very slowly he lowered it until it hung loosely from his hand and then he dropped to the floor. His mouth twitched and his eyes kept blinking. He went over to the couch and sat down.

"My wife," he said, "my wife was having her baby. She was in the hospital. Then this"—he motioned toward the window—"this thing happened. She was . . . she was so fragile— just a little thing." He held out his hands again as if groping for the right words. "She couldn't take the heat. They tried to keep her cool but . . . but she couldn't take the heat. The baby didn't live more than an hour and then . . . then she followed him." His head went down, and when he looked up again his eyes were wet. "I'm not a—I'm not a housebreaker. I'm a decent man. I swear to you—I'm a decent man. It's just that . . . well, this heat. This terrible heat. And all morning long I've been walking around the streets trying to find some water."

His eyes pleaded for understanding; and underneath the dirty sweat, his face suddenly looked young and frightened. "I didn't mean to do you any harm, honest. I wouldn't hurt you. Would you believe it?" He laughed. "I was scared of *you*. That's right—I was just as scared of you as you were of me."

He rose from the couch and started across the room, his foot hitting a fragment of the broken glass from the bottle. He looked down at it. "I'm . . . I'm sorry about that," he said. "I'm just off my rocker. I was just so thirsty." He moved toward the door past Mrs. Bronson. He held out a hand to her. It was a gesture that was almost supplication. "Please . . . please forgive me, will you? Will you please forgive me?"

He went to the door and leaned against the frame for a moment, the sweat pouring down his face. "Why doesn't it end?" he said in a low voice, almost unintelligible. "Why don't we just . . . why don't we just burn up?" He turned to them. "I wish it would end. That's all that's left now—just to have it end." He went out.

When Norma heard the front door close, she went over to Mrs. Bronson, helped her to her feet, and cradled her head in her arms, petting her like a mother.

"I've got a surprise for you," she said. "Mrs. Bronson, listen to me, I've got a surprise for you."

She went across the room and pulled out a canvas from a group of others. She turned it around and held it in front of her. It was a hurriedly done waterfall scene, obviously rough work and painted with desperation.

Mrs. Bronson looked at it for a long moment and slowly smiled. "It's beautiful, Norma. I've seen waterfalls like that. There's one near Ithaca, New York. It's the highest waterfall in this part of the country, and I love the sound of it." She went over to the canvas and touched it. "That clear water tumbling over the rocks—that wonderful clear water."

Suddenly she stopped and looked up, her eyes wide. "Did you hear it?" she asked.

Norma stared at her.

"Don't you hear it, Norma? Oh, it's a wonderful sound. It's so . . . it's so cool. It's so clear." She kept listening as she walked across the room to the window. "Oh, Norma," she said, her smile now a vapid, dreamy thing, "it's lovely. It's just lovely. Why, we could take a swim right now."

"Mrs. Bronson . . ." Norma said in a choked voice.

"Let's take a swim, Norma, at the bottom of the waterfall. I used to do that when I was a girl. Just sit there and let the water come down on you. Oh, the lovely water," she murmured, as she leaned her face against the burning-hot glass. "Oh, the beautiful water . . . the cool nice water . . . the lovely water."

The white-hot rays of the sun clawed at her face, and slowly she began to slump to the floor, leaving a patch of burnt flesh on the window, and then she crumpled in a heap silently.

Norma bent down over her. "Mrs. Bronson?" she said. "Mrs. Bronson?" Norma began to cry. "Oh, Mrs. Bronson . . ."

It happened rather quickly after that. The windows of the buildings began to crack and shatter. The sun was now the whole sky—a vast flaming ceiling that pressed down inexorably.

Norma had tried to pick up the gun but the handle was too hot to touch. Now she knelt in the middle of the room and watched as the paint began to run down the canvases, slow rivulets of thick sluggish color like diminutive lava streams; after a moment, they burst into flames that licked up the canvases in jagged, hungry assaults.

Norma didn't feel the pain when it finally came. She was not aware that her slip had caught fire or that liquid was running out from her eyes. She was a lifeless thing in the middle of an inferno, and there was nothing left inside her throat or mind to allow the scream to come out—

Then the building exploded and the massive sun devoured the entire city.

It was black and cold, and an icy frost lay thick on the corners of the window. A doctor with thin lips, his overcoat collar turned high, sat alongside the bed and reached over to touch Norma's forehead. He turned to look across the room at Mrs. Bronson, who stood by the door.

"She's coming out of it now," he said quietly. Then he turned back toward the bed. "Miss Smith?" There was a pause. "Miss Smith?"

Norma opened her eyes and looked up at him. "Yes," she whispered.

"You've been running a very high fever, but I think it's broken now."

"Fever?"

Mrs. Bronson moved to the bed. "You gave us a start, child—you've been so ill. But you're going to be all right now." She smiled hopefully at the doctor. "Isn't she, doctor? Isn't she going to be all right?"

The doctor didn't smile back. "Of course," he said quietly. Then he rose and motioned to Mrs. Bronson. He tucked the blankets tighter around the girl, picked up his bag, and moved out into the hall where Mrs. Bronson was waiting for him.

A cold air whistled up through the landing—and through

the window over the stairway snow came down in heavy ice-laden gusts.

"I hope she'll be all right," the doctor said to Mrs. Bronson. "Just let her sleep as much as she can." He looked down at his bag. "I wish I had something left to give her," he said disconsolately, "but the medicine's pretty much all gone now." He looked toward the window over the landing. "I'm afraid I won't be able to come back. I'm going to try to move my family south tomorrow. A friend of mine has a private plane."

Mrs. Bronson's voice was quiet and sad. "They say . . . they say on the radio that Miami is a little warmer."

The doctor just looked at her. "So they say." Then he stared at the ice-encrusted window. "But we're just prolonging it. That's all we're doing. Everybody running like scared rabbits to the south, and they say that within a week that'll be covered with snow down there, too."

Through the partially opened door to Mrs. Bronson's apartment a radio announcer's voice could be heard. "This is a traffic advisory," the voice said, "from the Office of Civil Defense. Motorists are advised to stay off the highways on all those routes leading south and west out of New York City. We repeat this advisory: *Stay off the highways!*"

The doctor picked up his bag and started toward the steps.

"There was a scientist on this morning," Mrs. Bronson said as she walked beside him. "He was trying to explain what happened. How the earth had changed its orbit and started to move away from the sun. He said that . . ." Her voice became strained. "He said that within a week or two—three at the most—there wouldn't be any more sun—that we'd all . . ." She gripped her hands together. *"We'd all freeze."*

The doctor tried to smile at her, but nothing showed on his face. He looked haggard and old and his lips were blue as he tightened the scarf around his neck, put on a pair of heavy gloves, and started down the steps.

Mrs. Bronson watched him for a moment until he disappeared around the corner of the landing, then she returned to Norma's room.

"I had such a terrible dream," Norma said, her eyes half closed. "Such an awful dream, Mrs. Bronson."

The older woman pulled a chair up closer to the bed.

"There was daylight all the time. There was a . . . a midnight sun and there wasn't any night at all. No night at all."

Her eyes were fully open now and she smiled. "Isn't it wonderful, Mrs. Bronson, to have darkness and coolness?"

Mrs. Bronson stared into the feverish face and nodded slowly. "Yes, my dear," she said softly, "it's wonderful."

Outside the snow fell heavier and heavier and the glass on the thermometer cracked. The mercury had gone down to the very bottom, and there was no place left for it to go. And very slowly night and cold reached out with frozen fingers to feel the pulse of the city, and then to stop it.

THE
RIP
VAN
WINKLE
CAPER

THE tracks of the Union Pacific were reptile twins snaking their way south of the Nevada line into the vast torrid valleys of the Mojave desert. And once a day when the crack streamliner, City of St. Louis, thundered along these tracks past the needle-like volcanic crags, the distant sawtoothed desolate mountains, the dead sea of ash and brittle creosote brush, it was the intrusion of a strange anachronism. The screaming power of the diesel pushed aside the desert winds. It shot past the white and arid wastes of the ancient land as if afraid of being caught by the jagged, crumbling spurs of rock that surrounded the great quadrangular desert.

And once . . . just once . . . the impossible happened. The steel cord that tied the train to the earth was parted. Too late, the giant wheels sent up protesting sparks and agonized metal shrieks, trying to stop that which could not be stopped —fifty tons of engine and train moving at ninety miles an hour. It thundered off the broken tracks and smashed against a slopping sand dune with an explosive roar that shattered that still desert with earth-shaking reverberation. Cars followed the engine off the tracks like nightmares piling atop nightmares until the carnage had spent itself. The City of St. Louis was a dying metal beast with fifteen broken vertebrae stretched across the desert floor.

The moving van lumbered up the side of the desert slope toward the lonely ledge above. It groaned and wheezed in the heat, while behind it a small sedan followed closely. When it reached the ledge the van pulled to the left and let the sedan go by, stopping a few hundred feet away. Then the van reversed until it had backed against the opening of a cave—a yawning mouth in the face of the rock. Two men got out of the van and two out of the sedan. They wore unmarked white coveralls, and all four met near the tailgate of the van. They were like a committee of quiet generals meeting for a critique after a giant battle—sweaty, dead-tired, but victorious.

What they had just accomplished *had* been a victory. It was an operation that needed the precision of a stop watch combined with the timing, logistics, and power of a full-scale invasion. And everything had worked beyond their wildest, most sanguine dreams. For inside the moving van, neatly piled in heavy motionless lumps, was two million dollars in gold bullion.

The tall man with the thin face and the steady, intelligent eyes, looked like a college professor. His name was Farwell and he had a doctorate in chemistry and physics. His specialty was noxious gasses. He turned toward the others and held up his thumb in a gesture of victory.

"Clockwork, gentlemen," he said with a thin smile. His eyes moved slowly left and right, staring into the faces of the other three.

Next him was Erbe, almost as tall as Farwell, with thin sloping shoulders, a pale nondescript face—perhaps a little younger-looking than his years. He was the expert in mechanical engineering. He could make anything, fix anything, manipulate anything. With probing eyes and surgeon's fingers, he would gently caress a maze of gears, cogs, wheels, cylinders—and coax them into a hum.

Alongside him was Brooks. Broad and stocky, partially bald, with an infectious grin and a Texas accent, he knew more about ballistics than almost anyone alive. Someone had said that his brains were made out of gunpowder, because in the area of firearms and other weaponry he was a dedicated genius.

And to his right was DeCruz—small, mercurial, handsome —a shock of unruly black hair hanging over deep-set, probing dark eyes. DeCruz was the expert in demolition. He was a master at destruction. He could improvise anything and blow up everything.

Two hours earlier these four men, in an incredible blending of talent, timing, and technique, had executed a heist unlike anything ever performed in the annals of crime. DeCruz had planted the five one-pound blocks of TNT that had blown up the tracks and sent the train to its destruction. Erbe had almost single-handedly put the two vehicles together from the parts of a dozen others—without parentage untraceable. Brooks had developed the grenades. And Farwell had come up with the sleeping gas. And in precisely thirteen minutes every occupant of the train had been asleep—the two engineers forever. Then the four men had moved quickly and quietly into one of the cars to remove the rotary-locked pouches carrying the bullion. Again DeCruz had utilized his talents to blow the locks apart, and the bullion had been transferred to the van.

It was part of their natures that none of them was concerned with the two dead engineers or the twenty-odd badly wounded human beings they'd left behind. Expediency was the one gospel that they all recognized and paid homage to.

It was DeCruz who hopped over the tailgate and started to push the treasure toward the rear of the van.

"Apples in the barrel," Erbe said, and he grinned as he started to carry one of the bars of bullion toward the cave.

Brooks took another bar of bullion and let his fingers run over it. "So far," he said; "but we ain't spent nothin' yet."

DeCruz paused and nodded thoughtfully. "Brooks is right. Two million dollars' worth of gold, but I'm still wearing dungarees and I got a dollar and twenty cents in my pocket."

Farwell chuckled and winked at them. "That's *this* year, Señor DeCruz. Today this . . ." He pointed to the tailgate and then nodded toward the cave opening. "But tomorrow! Tomorrow, gentlemen, like Croesus! Midas! Rockefeller and J. P. Morgan all rolled into one." He patted the gold piling up on the tailgate. "Perfection, gentlemen. That's how you performed. With perfection."

Brooks laughed. "Man, did you see that train engineer when he hit those brakes! Looked like he thought the world was comin' to an end."

"Why not?" DeCruz said, his voice shrill, his eyes flashing. He pointed to himself proudly. "When I blow up tracks, I blow up tracks!"

Brooks stared at him. There was a rooted dislike, an undisguised contempt in his look. "Find a foundry for me, DeCruz—I'll cast a medal for you."

DeCruz's black eyes returned the dislike. "What's *your* trouble, Brooks? That wasn't any easy thing tying up those tracks like that. You coulda done better, huh?"

Farwell, the catalyst, looked from one to the other. He motioned DeCruz back into the van. "May we get to business now?" he said. "We're on schedule and I'd like to keep it that way."

They continued to move the gold off the van and into the

cave. It was torturously hot and the ten-inch cubes were deadweight in their arms as they slowly emptied the van.

"Man!" said Brooks as he moved into the cave with the last of the bars. He put it on top of the pile next to the deep pit that had been dug days before. "You're a heavy little bastard. Any more at home like you?"

Erbe came up beside him. "Yeh, one million nine hundred and eighty thousand bucks' worth . . . just like him." He turned to Farwell. "It worked just like you said it would—car full of gold, train derailed, sleeping gas puts everybody out . . ." He looked down at the gas mask hanging from his belt. ". . . except us," he said pointedly.

Farwell nodded. "Except us, Mr. Erbe. It was not our time to sleep. It was our time to enrich ourselves." He looked briefly at his watch. "All right, gentlemen, the gold is in the cave. Next on the agenda—we destroy the van and Mr. Erbe wraps up the car with cosmoline."

He walked across the cave to the far end. There were four glass-covered boxes, the size of coffins, lined up evenly. Farwell touched the glass top of one of them and nodded his head approvingly.

"And now," he said in a whisper, "the *pièce de résistance* —the real culmination—the ultimate ingenuity."

The three men stood behind him in the shadows.

"It's one thing," Farwell's quiet voice continued, "to stop a train on its way from Los Angeles to Fort Knox and steal its cargo. It's quite another thing to remain free to spend it."

DeCruz squatted down in the dirt. "When?" he asked. "*When* do we spend it?"

"Don't you know, Señor DeCruz?" Farwell's voice was faintly disapproving. "I would have thought that this aspect of the plan would be particularly clear in your mind."

DeCruz rose and walked over to the glass boxes. He stared at them with obvious trepidation. "Rip Van Winkles," he said, "that's what we are . . ." He turned toward the others. "We're four Rip Van Winkles. I'm not sure—"

Farwell interrupted him. "What aren't you sure of, Mr. DeCruz?"

"Getting put to sleep, *Mr.* Farwell. Just lying down in these glass coffins and getting put to sleep. I like to know what I'm doing."

Farwell smiled at him. "You know what you're doing. I've explained it very precisely to you." He turned, taking the other men into his conversation. "All four of us will be placed in a state of suspended animation. A protracted . . .

rest, Mr. DeCruz. And when we wake up," he pointed toward the pit and the gold stacked alongside, "that's when we take our gold and enjoy it."

DeCruz turned from the glass box and faced him. "I say everybody should get their cut now and take his own chances!"

Brooks took out a large switchblade that gleamed in the dim light. "That's what *you* say, DeCruz." His voice was quiet. "But that ain't what we agreed on. What we agreed on was that we'd stash the gold here and then do what Farwell tells us to do. And so far he ain't been wrong. Not about anything. The train, the gold, the gas—everything. Just like he said. And all we had to do was walk over a lot of horizontal people and transfer a fortune like it was cotton candy."

"Amen to that," Erbe said.

"Amen to that, sure," DeCruz said excitedly, "but how about *this*!" He swiped at one of the boxes, with the back of his hand. "None of you mind being helpless and closed up in these?"

Brooks went very slowly over to DeCruz, the knife still held in his hand. "No, Mr. DeCruz," he said softly, "none of us mind."

The two men faced each other, and in this moment of challenge it was DeCruz who wavered and turned away. He continued to stare at the semi-opaque glass of the box, and he took a deep breath. "How long, Farwell?" he asked in a different voice. "When we each push the button inside and the gas comes out, and this . . . this suspended animation thing takes over. How long?"

"How long?" Farwell answered him softly. "I don't know exactly. I can only surmise. I would say that we would all wake up within an hour of each other—no more." He looked again down the long row of caskets. "I would say approximately one hundred years from today's date." He looked around the circle of faces. "One hundred years, gentlemen, and we shall walk the earth again." He turned and went over to the pit, then looked at the gold bullion. "As rich men, however," he continued, "as extremely rich men."

DeCruz's lips trembled. "One hundred years." He shut his eyes. "Just like Rip Van Winkle."

It took them the rest of the day to pile the gold into the hole and cover it with earth. The moving van was blown up with the last remaining block of TNT. The sedan was pulled into the cave, covered with cosmoline and then with a large tarpaulin. And then Farwell closed the giant steel door covering the opening, its outside a twin to the rock walls on either side.

The four men stood in the shadowy light of the lanterns set around the cave and their eyes were drawn to the four glass boxes that waited for them with quiet invitation. On a signal from Farwell each man climbed into his box, closed the lid, and locked it from inside.

"All right, gentlemen," Farwell said over the inter-com system linking the four boxes. "First of all, I want to know if you can hear me. Knock once on the side as I call your name." There was a pause. "DeCruz?"

DeCruz moved a shaking hand and knocked on the side of the glass.

"Erbe?"

There was a muffled sound from Erbe's coffin.

"Brooks?"

Brooks, grinning, tapped his fingers on the glass and tossed a salute.

The lantern light flickered weakly and the room was filled with an orange dusk in the last few moments before the darkness.

Farwell's voice was cool, deliberate. "Now I'm going to give you, in sequence, precisely what will happen," he said, his voice hollow in the silence. "First, you're to check the air locks located on your right. Do you see them there?"

Each man looked up to a spot just above his eyes.

"All right," Farwell's voice continued. "The red arrow should be pointed toward 'closed and locked.' Now you each count to ten very slowly. When you come to the end of the count, reach up with your left hand to the shelf just above your head. There's a small green button there. Do you all find it?"

There were movements within the other three coffins.

"You're to press this button. When that's done, you'll hear a slight hissing sound. That will be the gas being measured into the enclosures. Take three shallow breaths, then a long, deep one. After a moment you'll begin to experience a heavy, drowsy feeling. Don't fight this. Just continue to breathe regularly and try to remain as still as possible. A good idea would be to count backwards from twenty. This will occupy your mind and keep you from any excess movement. By the time you reach eight or seven you should lose consciousness."

There was another silence.

"All right," Farwell's voice continued. "Check your air locks first, gentlemen."

The other three men followed his directions, and then three sets of eyes turned in their confinement to look across the cave toward the first coffin.

"Now begin to count," Farwell's voice said, "and on ten, release the gas."

The lips of the four men moved as the quiet count-down took place—then, very slowly into each glass enclosure came a white stream of milky gas until the bodies inside were no longer visible.

"Good night, gentlemen." Farwell's voice was heavy and indistinct. "Pleasant dreams and a good sleep. I'll see you . . . in the next century." His voice became weaker. "In the next century, gentlemen."

There was no more movement and no more sound. The lamps around the cave flickered out and there was nothing but darkness.

Inside the glass caskets the four men breathed deeply and regularly, unconscious of the quiet *or* the darkness, oblivious now to the time passing outside the cave ninety miles from a wrecked train in the Mojave desert.

Time passed. The wrecked skeleton of the moving van turned brown with rust, and then disintegrated into little pieces of metal that mixed with the sand and was eaten by it. Winds blew; the sun crossed the sky day after day.

And time continued to pass, until there came a moment when a small lever inside the first glass box went "click" and the top started to open.

Farwell opened his eyes. For a moment he looked puzzled; gradually awareness flooded into his face. His body seemed heavy and sluggish and it was a while before he could move. Then very slowly he sat up and reached for a flashlight beside him. He had built this with a set of batteries of his own design, set in a welded case made of steel and magnesium. When he pushed the switch a beam of light shone up toward the ceiling of the cave. There was movement down the line as two other caskets opened and Brooks and DeCruz could be seen sitting up inside their caskets. The last box in line remained closed.

DeCruz climbed out of the box, his legs stiff and unfamiliar. There was a tremor in his voice. "It didn't work." He felt at his face, then moved his hand up and down his body. "We don't have any beards," he said. "Our nails haven't even grown." He stared accusingly at Farwell. "Hey! Master mind with the big brain and all the answers—*why didn't it work?*"

"It must have worked," Farwell said. "It was foolproof. All the body functions stopped—there wouldn't be any growth of beard or nails or anything else. I tell you, it worked. It *had* to work."

DeCruz moved across the dim cave and felt around the wall. He found a giant lever half surrounded by rocks. There was a clank of rusting chains, and after a moment the steel partition moved on its tracks. It let in blinding daylight that made the three men shut their eyes. It was several moments before they could become accustomed to the light. Then DeCruz walked out to the broad ledge and stared out over the horizon.

"Look," he said, his voice shaking, "there's the goddamn highway. It hasn't changed. It hasn't changed a bit." He whirled around, and grabbed Farwell by the shirt. "Master mind! Big brain! So instead of a hundred years, it's maybe an hour—and we're still hot. And all that gold back there is so much garbage, because everybody and his brother's going to be looking for it—"

Farwell flung off DeCruz's hand and turned around, staring back into the cave. "Erbe," he said. "We forgot Erbe."

The three men ran to Erbe's coffin. Farwell was the first to see what had happened. He picked up a large rock and stared at it. Then he looked up, first toward the ceiling and then down to the crack in the glass cover of the coffin.

"This is what did it," he said softly. "It cracked the glass and the gas escaped."

He looked down at the skeleton in the glass coffin.

"Mr. Erbe has proven my point, gentlemen. He's definitely proven my point . . . *the hard way.*"

Brooks and DeCruz stared. Neither of them spoke for a moment. Finally DeCruz asked, "How long . . . how long would it take"—he pointed toward the skelton—"for this to happen?"

Farwell made a gesture. "A year, or a hundred years." He looked toward the entrance to the cave. "But the odds are, Mr. DeCruz, that we're now in the year twenty sixty-one."

The three men walked into the sunlight.

"Now the next step, huh?" DeCruz's voice was urgent. "We get the gold into the car and we take it into the first city we find. And we either find a fence, or we melt it down some way." He faced Farwell. "That's the deal, isn't it?"

Farwell stared at him, and then looked at DeCruz's hands. There was something in the look that made DeCruz drop them to his sides.

"Why is it, Mr. DeCruz," Farwell asked him, "that greedy men are the most dreamless—the least imaginative—the stupidest?"

DeCruz's lips tightened. "Listen, Farwell—"

Farwell jerked his head toward the horizon. "For the first time, DeCruz," he interrupted him, "for the first time in the history of men we've taken a century and put it in our hip pockets. We've taken a lease on life and outlived our stay. We've had our cake, but we're still going to eat it." His voice became thoughtful and quieter. "That's quite an adventure out there, Mr. DeCruz. Though you're a little insensitive to it, that's quite an adventure. That's a world we've never seen before. A brand-new exciting world we'll move into."

DeCruz's features twisted. "But with gold, Farwell," he said, "with two million bucks' worth of gold. That's how we're going to move into it."

"Of course," Farwell said quietly. "Of course." He continued to stare across the vast expanse of desert. "I wonder what kind of a world . . ."

He turned and went slowly across the ledge toward the cave, conscious of this incredible moment; feeling an almost wild exuberance as his awareness whispered to him that they, of all men, had conquered time.

DeCruz followed him and began to scrabble in the pit. Each time he found another bar of gold, he gave an exclamation of excitement and joy. Brooks helped him, and the two men shared enthusiasm as they continued their digging.

But to Farwell the gold seemed no longer important. He watched them pile it up and then remove the cosmoline from the car. There was a tense moment when DeCruz sat in the front seat and turned the ignition key. The car engine roared back to life. It purred as if it had been parked not an hour ago—a belated testament to the dead Erbe's efficiency. But Farwell was only vaguely aware of the engine noise or of the gold being loaded. What preoccupied him was what lay beyond the desert, beyond what they could see—the hidden new world waiting for exploration.

DeCruz shut off the ignition and asked, "All set?"

Farwell looked at him. "All loaded?"

DeCruz nodded. "She's all ready." He turned away, his eyes unsubtle reservoirs of deception. "Maybe," he suggested, "I oughta drive her up and down a little. See if she runs okay."

Brooks, stripped to the waist, sweat pouring from him, took a step over toward the car. "Ain't you the most thoughtful little fella that ever come down a pike! You wanna take her for a little ride, huh," he mimicked, "and see if she's okay. Just you and the gold. Why, I wouldn't trust you with gold if it was the filling in your own mother's tooth. No, buddy boy—when we move outta here, we move out together." He turned to Farwell. "Where's the water can? We might as well load that up."

Farwell pointed toward it a hundred feet away. "It's over there where we buried Erbe," he said.

Brooks nodded and started across the sand toward the metal can that sat beside a freshly filled grave.

DeCruz watched him, his eyes narrowed. He very carefully and unobtrusively turned on the ignition key and started up the engine.

Farwell was closing the entrance to the cave when he saw the car shoot ahead across the ledge. Brooks saw it at the same moment and his initial surprise gave way to a wild fear as he saw the car, like some malevolent beast, close in on him.

"DeCruz!" he screamed. "DeCruz! You dumb bastard—"

DeCruz's eyes remained set, focused directly in front of him, staring through the windshield. He saw Brooks make a frantic sideways leap—but too late. He heard the thump of metal hitting, jarring, tearing. And with it the scream of the mangled man. He let the car surge forward, keeping his foot on the accelerator. Then he glanced over his shoulder to see Brooks' body face down in the sand a hundred feet behind him. He took his foot off the accelerator and put it on the brake.

Nothing happened. DeCruz's throat constricted as he realized the far ledge was only a few yards ahead of him. Again he slammed on the brake, and reached desperately, frantically, for the emergency. Too late. The car was doomed, and it was during the few seconds before it plunged over the far ledge that DeCruz managed to open the door and fling himself out. The impact knocked the breath from him and he felt sand, harsh and gritty, in his mouth. And at the same time he heard the sound of the car smashing hundreds of feet below against the rocks.

DeCruz got to his feet and went over to the far end of the ledge, staring down at the car, which now looked like a toy destroyed in a child's fit of anger. He looked back at Farwell, who was standing over Brooks's broken body. Their eyes met and Farwell came over to him.

"DeCruz . . . DeCruz, what in God's name!" Farwell looked down at the car lying on its side, and then back toward the dead man. "Why?" he whispered. "Tell me. *Why?*"

DeCruz stared back intently into Farwell's face. "Brooks had an accident . . . or hadn't you noticed?"

"Why did he have an accident? Why did you do it?"

DeCruz nodded perfunctorily at the car. "That I didn't plan to do. I wanted Brooks dead—not the car." Then, challenge in his voice: "Dead weight, Farwell. So much dead weight."

He smiled, the corners of his thin mouth drew up—and Farwell noted the evil of his face. He remembered when DeCruz had joined them. This was the one man who would bear watching, he had thought. But he had remembered too late.

He looked at the battered body of Brooks, half buried by the sand, both legs sticking out at incredible angles. Too late for Brooks. Again he looked into the dark eyes that continued to challenge him. Maybe too late for himself too. He turned deliberately and started to walk back toward the cave. "I keep underestimating you, Mr. DeCruz," he said as he went.

"Farwell!" DeCruz shouted at him.

Farwell stopped without turning around.

"We do it my way now, huh? Take all we can put in two knapsacks and then hit the road."

Farwell was silent for a moment as his mind worked. Then he shrugged. "I can't think of any other alternative at the moment." He thought of the car far down in the gorge lying on its side, then he began to laugh. "The obvious," he chuckled. "The simple idiotic ridiculous obvious."

He laughed again and kept shaking his head as DeCruz stared at him, puzzled. "Even if it had run, Mr. DeCruz," he explained, "even if you hadn't wrecked it"—he motioned toward the gorge—"the license plates are a hundred years old. We would've been picked up the moment we hit the highway." He chuckled again, this time more softly, and looked up at the hot sun. "We'll load what we can, but it's going to be very warm walking. Very warm."

He smiled at DeCruz. "So you're quite right, Mr. DeCruz. Now we'd better hit the road."

The two men walked for hours down the sandy slopes toward the highway. They plodded along silently, each carrying a knapsack full of gold bullion; each feeling the hot sun beating down on them. Early in the afternoon they reached Highway 91. It crossed the flats of Ivanpah Lake, running east and west. Farwell and DeCruz paused briefly on one of its shoulders, and it was Farwell who pointed east. They hoisted their knapsacks higher and started walking along the side of the road.

An hour later, Farwell, stumbling, held up his hand and stood there slumped over—his face a red mask of pain and deadening fatigue. "Hold it up, DeCruz," he said, breathing heavily. "I've got to rest."

DeCruz looked at him and smiled. Anything that took strength, will, resolve, resilience—this was what he understood and could conquer. He was a young animal with no breaking point. "How're you doing, Farwell?" he asked with an enigmatic smile.

Farwell nodded, not wanting to talk, his eyes glazed with overexertion. "The map said . . . the map said twenty-eight miles to the next town. At this rate we won't reach it until tomorrow afternoon sometime."

DeCruz continued to smile. "At this rate, you may *never* reach it. I told you you should've stayed back there and watched the gold. I kept telling you, Farwell."

This time it was Farwell who smiled. "Oh, yes—you did, didn't you, Mr. DeCruz?" His own smile now was twisted. "But I don't think I'd have ever seen you again. I think I'd have died back there."

He looked down the limitless stretch of highway and his eyes narrowed. "There hasn't been a car," he said thoughtfully, "not a single car." He let his eyes scan the distant row of mountains and there was a hint of incipient terror creeping into his voice. "I hadn't thought of that. I hadn't even thought of that. Just like with the license plates. What if—"

"What if what?" DeCruz's voice was harsh.

Farwell stared at him. "What's happened these past one hundred years, DeCruz? What if there's been a war? What if they dropped a bomb? What if this highway stretched to—" He didn't finish. He simply sat down on the sandy shoulder of the road and removed his knapsack, turning his head from side to side as if trying to slough off the heavy weight of heat and sun and the desperate tiredness.

DeCruz came up close to him. "Stretched to what?" he said, and his voice sounded frightened.

Farwell half closed his eyes. "Stretched to nothing, DeCruz. Stretched to nothing at all. Maybe there *isn't* any town up ahead. Maybe there *aren't* any people." He began to laugh, shaking uncontrollably until he fell over on his side and lay there, the laughter still pouring out of him.

DeCruz shook him, then took hold of him and forced him upright. "Knock it off, Farwell!" he said tightly. "I told you to knock it off!"

Farwell looked into the dirty, sweaty face that was close to hysteria and shook his head. "You're a frightened little man, aren't you, DeCruz? You've always been a frightened little man. But it's not your fear that disturbs me. It's your greed. It's because you're so greedy that you have no appreciation of irony. None at all. And wouldn't that be the irony of *all* ironies to walk until our hearts burst, carrying all this gold."

He stopped abruptly as a distant sound suddenly broke the quietness of the desert. It was so faint that at first Farwell thought it might be his imagination. But it grew in intensity until it took on its own dimension. DeCruz heard it too, then, and both men looked up toward the sky. First it was a speck, and the speck became a form—a jet aircraft with a vapor trail stretched across the blue desert sky. Then it disappeared far off in another direction.

This time DeCruz laughed. "There's a world left, Farwell," he said triumphantly. "That proves it. And that means there's a city up ahead. And we're gonna make it, buddy. We're gonna make it. Come on, Farwell, let's get moving."

He went back to his own knapsack and hoisted it to his shoulder; then he reached down for his canteen, uncorked the top, and took a long gurgling drink, the rivulets of water pouring down his chin as he sucked greedily on it. But halfway through his enjoyment he took a look at Farwell and smiled.

Farwell's hand had rested on his belt, but now he was staring down at a small chain attached to nothing. Farwell looked up. His voice shook. "My canteen came loose," he said. "I must've left it back on the dunes the last place we stopped. I don't have any water."

He tried to keep his voice even—his face unrevealing; but

no pretense, however subtle, could cloak this kind of reality. He knew it, and the thin smile playing on DeCruz's face told him that his companion was well aware of it.

DeCruz hoisted his knapsack higher on his back. "That's tragic, Mr. Farwell," he said, the smile persisting. "That's the saddest story I've heard all day."

Farwell wet his lips. "I need water, DeCruz. I need it desperately."

DeCruz's face took on a look of exaggerated concern. "Water, Mr. Farwell?" He looked around like a bad actor. "Why, I believe there's some water around that you could drink." He looked down, farce-like in his concern, at his own canteen. "Why—here's water, Mr. Farwell." He looked across the shimmering heat at the parched face of the older man. "One drink—one bar of gold. That's the price."

"You're out of your mind," Farwell said, his voice cracking. "You're out of your goddamned mind."

"One drink—one bar of gold." DeCruz's smile faded. These were the ground rules and he was laying them out.

Farwell stared at DeCruz, and then slowly reached into his knapsack, hoisting out a gold bar. He threw this on the road. "I continue to underrate you, Mr. DeCruz," he said. "You're quite an entrepreneur."

DeCruz shrugged, unscrewed the cap of his canteen, and carried it over to him. "Ain't it the truth, Mr. Farwell," he said, offering the canteen.

Farwell started to drink, but after a few swallows DeCruz pulled the canteen away from him. "One drink—one bar of gold," he said. "That's the going rate today, Mr. Farwell. It may go up tomorrow. I haven't checked the market. But for today, it's one for one." Then, in a different tone, the tone of a man who's suddenly taken charge, "Let's go, Mr. Farwell!"

He jammed Farwell's gold bar into his own knapsack, turned abruptly, and started down the highway. Over his shoulder he could see Farwell stumble to his feet, dragging the knapsack along the road like some recalcitrant pet reluctant to follow him.

At four o'clock in the afternoon Farwell felt that he could no longer breathe. His heart was like a lump of lead smashing back and forth inside his body. The late afternoon sun stayed hot and persistent as it slowly nose-dived toward a distant mountain peak.

DeCruz, several yards ahead of Farwell, turned to smile at him. It was his voice that Farwell could no longer stand. The corroding contempt in it, the insufferable superiority of the strong surveying the weak.

"What's the matter, Farwell?" DeCruz asked. "You poopin' out already? Hell, we've got another four or five hours of daylight."

Farwell stopped and shook his head. His lips were cracked, and just to touch them with the salt-tipped end of his tongue was a torture. "Stop," he said, his voice a mumble. "Have to stop. . . . Need water, DeCruz. . . . Must have water." He stood there swaying on his feet, his eyes sunk back in his head.

DeCruz grinned at him. It had reached the point where the gold actually meant nothing to him. What was of the essence was his perogative. The juxtaposition of leader and follower dictated now not by brains but by the elements. He stood over Farwell, enjoying the other man's agony. "I've got about a quarter of a canteen left, Farwell," he said. He held up the canteen and shook it, then took a drink. "That's good," he said, the water driveling out of the corners of his mouth. "That was very good."

Farwell held out a shaking hand. "Please, DeCruz," he said through cracked lips, his words coming out distorted from a swollen tongue. "Please . . . help me."

DeCruz deliberately held the canteen up. "The rate of exchange has changed a little bit this afternoon, Mr. Farwell. It's two bars of gold—for one swallow."

Farwell's legs gave out and he sank to his knees on the ground. He slowly, painstakingly, removed the knapsack from around his neck and with a massive effort spilled out the gold bars. There were four left. He was unable to lift the two in his hand and finally wound up pushing them across the sand over toward the other man. DeCruz lifted them easily and put them into his knapsack. The weight of them started a tear along one side, but this was of no concern to DeCruz. He looked down at the bulging container, and then into the face of Farwell. He could see the hatred behind the tired eyes and, perversely, this pleased him.

"You angry, Mr. Farwell?" he asked smoothly. "You're not angry, are you?"

Farwell did not speak. He very slowly, with thick, sweaty fingers, tied up his knapsack and then rolled over to lie on his side, his breath coming in tortured gusts from an overworked set of lungs in a body pushed beyond its endurance.

They slept the night, and at seven in the morning started out again. DeCruz's stamina was unchanging, and he deliberately set a pace too fast for Farwell, who stumbled and lurched behind him. Several times DeCruz paused and looked back over his shoulder, smiling. Twice he took a drink of water, doing in flamboyantly and obviously until the moment Farwell came up beside him; then he screwed on the cap and hurried ahead.

Farwell was like a ghost—dead, lusterless eyes set in a filthy sand-covered face, lips and skin cracked like some aged parchment.

At noon the sun was a broiling mass overhead and Farwell suddenly turned white and dropped to his knees. DeCruz waited for him, but he saw that this time the older man was not getting up. He walked over to him and pushed him with his foot.

"Farwell?" he asked. There was a pause. The man looked lifeless. "Come on, Farwell. We've got some miles to go yet."

A groan came from the man on the ground. He lifted his head, his eyes closed, his mouth open, his swollen tongue off to one side. "No." The voice came like an animal's. "No," he said again. "I can't go any further. I need water."

DeCruz chuckled and handed him the canteen. "One swallow, Mr. Farwell. One swallow."

Farwell's hands trembled as he gripped the canteen and put it to his mouth. He could hear the water swishing inside, and all his instincts, all his desires—the absolute key to his own survival—were funneled into this one action as he put it to his lips. DeCruz's hand came down hard and swift, pushing the canteen away. Its top gashed Farwell's tender lips, drawing blood, as he looked up unbelieving.

"We hadn't figured out the contract, Mr. Farwell," DeCruz said, his eyes two dark pinpoints. "Today the rate's gone up again."

Farwell's eyes were almost closed, as painfully, he took the knapsack from around his neck and let it drop to the ground. He kicked it across.

DeCruz chuckled and went down on his knees to retrieve it. In doing so, his own knapsack was left in the road and one of the gold bars spilled out of it as it tilted over. His back was to Farwell as he started to pick up the gold.

Farwell stared at him, marveling that he could feel hatred at this moment—that he could feel anything beyond his own suffering. But the hatred brought awareness that this was the final moment, his last chance.

He stared at DeCruz's broad back, hating its youth, hating the muscles that rippled underneath the shirt, hating the fact that DeCruz was going to win, while he himself would succumb. He felt his anger surging underneath, and for just one instant it dredged up strength and resolve. His fingers closed on a gold bar and he slowly lifted it. Then, rising to his feet, somehow incredibly, he managed to raise the gold bar high. He lurched sideways at DeCruz, just as the other man looked up at him. Farwell let the bar drop from his hands. It struck DeCruz on the temple.

DeCruz let out one small gasp and fell backwards. Again Farwell picked up the bar and let it smash into DeCruz's upturned face. This time there was a crunching sound as DeCruz's skull caved in. And through the bloody mangled face the eyes looked up. They retained the last emotion the man ever felt. Surprise. Absolute, incredulous surprise.

Farwell felt weakness return to him. He stood there wavering, his legs like rubber bands, his body a mass of pain. He turned and stumbled over to the canteen that was lying on its side. The water had spilled out into the sand. The canteen was empty.

Farwell started to cry, the tears coursing down his filthy beard-stubbled face. He fell to his knees, his shoulders shaking, his fingers caressing the empty canteen—as if he might be able to milk liquid from it.

After a while he got to his feet, looked at the gold bars spread out around him, and shook his head. They were meaningless lumps of dead weight. But he knew that they were all that remained to him. He went down on his knees again and struggled with them, trying to pick them up, then trying to push them across the sand toward the knapsacks. But he had no more strength left and it was only with a superhuman effort that he was finally able to lift one up by cradling it against his body and hoisting it with both arms. This one he carried with him down the highway—a lurching stumbling figure of a man who moved by reflex and nothing else. There was no liquid left in throat or mouth, and each breath he took was a hot bolt of pain coursing through his body. But still he walked and continued to walk until late afternoon.

He fainted, and was unaware of the side of his face hitting a rock as he pitched forward. He just lay there, his eyes closed, feeling a dreamy contentment flow over him. Then he forced his eyes open as he heard the sound. First it was a distant indistinct hum, then it became the sound of an engine. He tried to move his arms and legs, but they were beyond command now. Only his eyes had life. He tried to turn his head, but it was only his eyes that moved, and through one corner he could see an approaching vehicle—a metallic low-slung thing that shrieked toward him and then slowed down, the noise cutting off abruptly.

He heard footsteps cross the road over to him and he looked up. It was a tall man in a loose-fitting garment, but the figure was hazy and indistinct; and Farwell could not get his swollen tongue or cracked lips to function. He felt terror as he realized that no words were coming from him. But then, from deep inside him, came a voice. It was like the sound of a record player slowly running down. The words were grotesque and almost unformed, but they came out.

"Mister . . . mister . . . this is gold here. This is real gold. I'll give it to you if you'll drive me into town. If you'll give me water. I must have water." He forced one hand to move across the sand where it pointed to that last bar of gold a few feet from him. "Gold," the voice came again. "It's real gold. And you can have it. I'll give it to you. I'll give it to you. . . ." The fingers clutched convulsively, and suddenly the hand opened. There was a spasmodic jerk, and then there was no movement at all.

The man knelt down to listen for Farwell's heart beat. When he rose to his feet he shook his head. "Poor old guy," he said. "I wonder where *he* came from."

The woman in the vehicle rose from her seat to look across the road. "Who is it, George?" she asked. "What's the matter with him?"

The man walked back to the vehicle and got into the driver's seat. "Some old tramp," he said, "that's who it *was*. He's dead now."

The woman looked at the gold bar in her husband's hand. "What's that?"

"Gold. That's what he said it was. Wanted to give it to me in exchange for a ride into town."

"Gold?" The woman wrinkled her nose. "What in the world is he doing with gold?"

The man shrugged. "I don't know. Off his rocker, I guess. Anybody walking in this desert at this time of day *would* be off his rocker." He shook his head and held up the bar of gold. "Can you imagine that? Offered that as if it was worth something."

"Well, it was worth something once, wasn't it? Didn't people use gold as money?"

The man opened the door. "Sure—a hundred years ago or so, before they found a way of manufacturing it." He looked at the heavy dull metal in his hand and then threw it onto the shoulder of the road. He closed the door. "When we get back into town we'll have the police come back and pick him up." He pushed a button on the dashboard, setting the automatic driver control, then looked over his shoulder at the figure of Farwell, who lay in the sand like a scarecrow blown down by the wind. "Poor old guy," he said thoughtfully, as the vehicle started to move slowly forward. "I wonder where he came from." He put his hands behind his head and closed his eyes.

The woman pushed another button and a glass top slid forward, shutting off the heat. The vehicle started down the highway, and after a moment disappeared.

Fifteen minutes later a police helicopter arrived, hovered over the scene, and landed. Two uniformed men walked over to the body of Farwell, gently placed it on a stretcher, and carried it over to the aircraft. The officer in charge noted down on a small pad the particulars. "Unidentified man. Age approximately sixty. Death from overexposure and exhaustion." Three scrawled lines on a policeman's pad, and it comprised the obituary for one Mr. Farwell, a Doctor of Chemistry and Physics.

Weeks later they found DeCruz's body, almost decomposed; and not long after, the body of Brooks and the skeleton of Erbe.

All four men were minor mysteries, and their bodies were consigned to the earth without mourning and without identity. The gold was left where it lay—stretched across the desert and piled up in the back seat of a disintegrating ancient car. It soon became imbedded in the landscape, joined the sage, saltbrush, pearlweed and the imperishable cacti. Like Messrs. Farwell, Erbe, Brooks, and DeCruz, it had no value. No value at all.